MENAGERIE IN THE DARK

STORIES

CHRIS KAUZLARICH

PHANTOM QUILL
PRESS

BOOKS BY CHRIS KAUZLARICH

A Phantom Quill Press book.

Published by Phantom Quill Press 2025

Published by Phantom Quill Press, a division of CK Phantom Quill LLC, Naples, FL 34119.

Phantom Quill Press and the colophon are registered trademarks of CK Phantom Quill LLC.

Names: Kauzlarich, Chris (author).

Title: Menagerie in the Dark: Stories / Chris Kauzlarich.

Identifiers: ISBN 979-8-9986793-0-8 (hardcover) | ISBN 979-8-9986793-1-5 (paperback) | ISBN 979-8-9986793-2-2 (ebook)

www.chriskauzlarich.com

Jacket and cover design by @GermanCreative on Fiverr.

Human Authored™, Reg #: 9458385, https://authorsguild.org/human

 Formatted with Vellum

For Buck and Laverne.
I'll never let the void take you.

MENAGERIE IN THE DARK

PART ONE
DUSK

A DREAM OF INNOCENCE

He ran down the uneven lane. Beautiful archways and Renaissance-style porticos surrounded him in a panorama of splendor. The city was perfect: an amalgamation of fifteenth-century Florence and Imperial Venice. It was home. It was safety.

Rumble.

Flash.

The boy lost his footing as the ground quaked beneath his feet, the force throwing him face down onto the cobblestones. White spots, like stars, danced before his eyes, an unexpected meteor shower that sprung to life just for him. A warmth rolled down his face, and he swiped at it, trying to push it away. His hand came away red, a startling shock in a place that hadn't ever shown violence. Blood, his life's essence displayed for the world to see.

Rumble.

Flash.

He stood, unsure of his balance, as another tremor subsided. The boy could not comprehend what was happening to his city, his sanctuary. Vast sections of stone were now strewn across his path, toppled and smashed into mere fragments of their former selves as if hurled by a trebuchet. High pieces were now low. The city was changing. It was under siege, a crack in the facade resembling the blemish on the boy's face.

He started running again, away from the damage, away from the change.

Rumble.

Flash.

He caught the marble railing along the canal as his foot slid from under him, a stumble that resulted in a bloodied knee. Something was wrong. This place had never done this. It had always been benign. Gentle. At peace.

A roar erupted from below, a sound concocted in nightmares. He caught his breath, hoping whatever it was wouldn't find him. Despite his trepidation, he peered over the rail.

The canal was gone, replaced by the ground far below; the city was in the air, an island racing toward the clouds in the hope of salvation.

Rumble.

Flash.

He straightened, straining to see over the edge. A bellow that could shatter worlds met him with hot, concussive force. The boy froze at the sight of the fiery maw below. Tentacles of flame lashed upward as if from hell, reaching for the city as it tried to escape. There was no hope; they moved too slowly. The street groaned as the conflagration whipped at the island's underbelly, loosening large chunks of earth that plummeted into the inferno beneath him. He didn't know where to go or which direction to flee. A massive cupola split atop the building behind him while the ground heaved like an animal in its last moments, the searing heat melting the bedrock.

Scraping.

Explosions.

Heat.

. . .

Wailing.
Sirens.
Pain...

The last rumble.
The last flash.
Darkness...

"COME ON, WAKE UP, SON," an officer said, kneeling next to the boy, wiping the hair back from his face.

He tried to breathe and coughed instead, heat racing through his chest with each exhalation. A loud crackle followed by shouts erupted behind him; he turned to look, stiff and covered in soot. A brick apartment building was blazing, smoke pluming upward, filling the air with its black malevolence.

The boy sat up on the pavement but crouched stiffly, frozen in place, a hoarse, raspy sound emanating from his lips. Something was wrong; this place was wrong. He looked to his left, and two paramedics were zipping up charred remains in a body bag, a single scorched hand poking out to meet the glow of the spotlights—the nails were painted, their pastel blue hue unmistakable against the darkened flesh of the fingers.

"Mommy...," the boy croaked as tears rolled down his cheeks. Black streams polluted his face as ash collected in the salty anguish of his soul. He started to move, as if to reach out and grab the solitary hand, that last visible piece of his mother, but was impeded by a blast of debris that landed near him like shrapnel as the building gave another great rumble, the mighty sentinel in its death throes. He lifted his arm to shield his face from the assault, and from the reality of what he'd just seen.

His home was broken. The boy recalled all the days he had explored the hallways, imagining the quests each new turn would bring as the complex became his paradise. The stairwells stood tall and austere, their many steps towering to new heights, and the laundry rooms acted as hidden labyrinths. Whether playing tag with the other children or evading the bully from the twelfth floor, the dragon to his knighthood, those walls were his. His Camelot, in his city. And at the center of it all was his mom, who he could always go home to in apartment 403. And now it was all gone.

Another officer walked past, tilting his cap to the boy, face glum and covered in the building's marrow, gray and smudged.

The boy looked into the officer's eyes, the one with his arms wrapped around him. His smile was flat, meant to be reassuring, but it hid nothing.

He looked back to the body bag, his mother's hand sealed beneath its thick plastic, the bright Easter pastel polish dimmed forever. She had just painted them that morning while he colored eggs. *We'll match,* she had said, her little pieces of joy to give him just a bit of comfort.

"Mommy..."

"I know, little guy... I know," said the officer, lifting and holding him tightly as he carried him to an ambulance.

The tears came faster. His home was no more. There was no more safety. His dreams were shattered. The boy already knew that nobody would be left to care for him if something happened to his mother; his grandma had just died a few weeks before.

I promise this will be a good Easter, sweetie. We'll say a prayer for Grandma. How does that sound? It'll be okay because we have each other. Right?

He had nodded vigorously, cuddling into his mother's arms. She was his rock. She'd never leave him alone. *I love you to the moon and back.*

He clenched the officer tighter.

"Hey," the officer said, returning the boy's squeeze. "We'll take care of you, alright?" he continued. "She's still with you. I promise. And we... we'll make sure you aren't alone."

Something snapped inside the boy; a part untethered as his safety line lost its hold, plunging him into this new existence. He had all the confirmation he needed as the man's hollow words rang in his ears. A dream of innocence was destroyed as the nightmare of reality was born. Mommy was gone.

"To the moon and back...."

BETRAYED HEART

"She's out getting fucked again," I said to nobody in particular, unable to hold back. I paced the kitchen, eyes moving from side to side, counting the floor tiles with each step.

Twenty-nine: I knew that number by heart at this point. I even knew tiles thirteen and nineteen had small cracks; their contours seared into my brain. I checked the clock, a constant loop like Groundhog Day.

My hand trembled, the physical manifestation of my loss of control and the unfortunate effects of too much coffee.

Why did she do this to me—no, *to us*?

Everything had been going so well, but on reflection, I knew this was my delusion. I allowed this to happen. Our engagement wasn't the smoothest experience of my life, but I buried the uncertainty under layers of hope and fantasy. Our first date was better, though; it seemed more sure.

Gosh, what had it been, ten years? We had gone to Blue Jay's, an upscale burger joint, at least by still-unemployed college graduate standards. It wasn't exactly the classiest option, but for my budget, it fit with its sheet metal walls and circular diner booths—retro but private with five-dollar beers and the sizzling hum of oil on the flat grill.

We had already known each other by the time of this first "official" date, but it had been years since we'd seen each other. And when I saw her walk into the restaurant from my seat in a booth, she looked even more beautiful than I remembered from the first day we'd met—sitting on the distressed leather couch at our mall's Abercrombie & Fitch, waiting for the manager to begin orientation.

It shouldn't be a surprise to anyone that we both worked there, considering how they used to be, selling catalogs with dicks and tits in them and an atmosphere rife with discrimination. It was superficial as hell, which was us: superficial and clueless. We'd had chemistry. I could feel the sparks every time we spoke, each conversation laced with suggestion and tension.

That wasn't our time, though. She'd had a boyfriend who worked with us, a jock who would have fit in perfectly on *Jersey Shore*, so we talked and occasionally flirted, but for the most part, I kept my distance, not wanting to get on his bad side—I wasn't his level of fit. The bulging vein in his forehead was warning enough.

We promised to keep in touch as we left that job and our hometown for college—she going to the other side of the country while I stayed within two hours—connecting on Facebook when it was trendy and had its uses other than spreading misinformation. Over time, communication broke down to those rare occasions when one of us congratulated or encouraged the other as our relationship statuses ebbed and flowed from single to taken. Time and location weren't on our side, at least not until we each graduated and she moved back home.

> HER
>
> Hey, I hope all is well. We should get together sometime. Here's my new number—just wanted to make sure you had it. Keep in touch.

That's right. She sent me her number. Why did she want me to have it? Unless... I may have read into it more than I should have, but I took it as destiny. After all that time dreaming of what could have been, she *wanted* me to keep in touch. She went out of her way to send me her phone number. I didn't hesitate.

And that's what brought us to the burger joint. I waved, and she hurried over to sit across from me, her blonde hair cut short and cheeks pink. She was still little Charli, everyone's nickname for her, as she was a dead ringer for Charlize Theron except five-foot-two instead of Charlize's five-ten.

We smiled at each other, but she couldn't meet my gaze, a shyness I didn't remember. I didn't blame her; my shirt was sticking to my back with my own anxiety kicking in. The dinner proceeded this way, us reminiscing but eye contact a rarity. I took it as a good sign, a deep-seated attraction that brought out this new dynamic between us. I followed her lead, being just as bashful and finding comfort in it. I didn't know if I could be as forward as she needed, not with her. At least not yet.

Dinner ended too soon, even though we'd been there for over two hours. The summer night was hot and humid, the Midwest's finest, and as we walked through the parking lot, the first of many romance tropes that seemed to weave itself into our relationship developed its first stitch; rain began to fall, so heavy it was like a bucket turned over, dumping onto us as we fled to my car as it was the closest means of salvation. My feet slid and squished in my leather flip-flops, causing several near falls as I struggled to open my car door, mentally kicking myself for not being gallant and opening hers. Luckily for me, we were both focused on the end game: getting out of the rain.

The windows fogged as we sat there, giggling and soaked, as the unexpected thunderstorm raged around us for almost a half hour. I want to say something more happened, that I finally got my courage and went for it, but we were too unsure around each other, or maybe it was just puppy love, I'm not sure which. Regardless, when I'd finally mustered up the courage to attempt a kiss, the rain stopped, and my hand only had the chance to brush hers as she reached for the door handle. I'd missed my chance, but it was a start.

She texted me later that night, telling me it was great to see me and she hoped we could get together again soon. I responded clumsily, never being a fan of texting since, at the time, T9 was the only way to type unless you had a Blackberry; I wasn't that fortunate. I pushed to get together again during the upcoming weekend. To my relief, she said yes.

That was the seed, our beginning. Two weeks later, we'd already had five dates. My dream girl and I were sprouting into something.

Speaking of something, that first time... that was special. She had been at my house (well, my parents' house, my temporary lodging, having just graduated from college) after we'd been out to the movies. It seemed that date six would be the lucky number. We went to my room. It was nothing special but sizable, with enough space to fit a small loveseat, leftover from my college dorm, and we'd started to make out, *Friends* playing on the TV in the background.

My hands slipped up her thigh, squeezing her ass. I'd inhaled her scent; something new and unfamiliar but etched in my mind as distinctly hers. Her hands moved just as deftly, caressing my arms, back, and pecs. We were bound to each other, leaving no space between us but the thin fabric of our summer attire. I craved her, and not just that night but for the preceding five years.

We moved to the bed, me hoisting her up in my arms as she wrapped her legs around me, pulling her pelvis into my hardness.

Everything seemed to move more frantically, yet oddly in stasis. I know that doesn't make sense, but time seemed to accelerate with us rubbing, groping, and gyrating, yet our clothes remained intact as if there was no forward momentum. I wanted it so desperately, yet I couldn't be the one to remove that first article of clothing, not even lowering the strap of her camisole from her shoulder. She moaned, reaching her hand along my abs before brushing her hand lower along my girth. The time had come, finally.

I began unzipping my shorts and, as if breaking some kind of trance—the sound of the little metal teeth shattering the silence like a freshly engaged chainsaw—the lust left her eyes, replaced by, I don't know, panic?

She fled, telling me sorry, she had to go. I'd pushed it. I'd gone too far. The last thing I ever wanted to do was to scare her away or give her the feeling that I was pressuring her. I'd known too many guys like that in college, seeing women as nothing more than conquests. Was I that guy?

I was stunned, letting it sink in. I'd blown my shot.

Thirty minutes passed, and then I heard from her. Honestly, I felt a little ashamed for not reaching out to her first.

> HER
>
> I'm sorry about tonight.

I was taken aback. After all, it had been me, hadn't it? I tried to remain hopeful.

> What do you mean? Sorry about what? I just hope you're okay.

> I'm fine, just a little embarrassed, you know, that it didn't happen. I don't want to rush this. I think I've done that too many times—rushed things, I mean.

I let out a long breath, releasing a burst of stars in my vision from the lack of oxygen. We still had a chance! No matter how much time she needed, I could wait.

> Oh my God, no worries at all. I'm just glad you're okay. See you tomorrow?

> Yes :)

I can't describe the relief I'd felt in that moment. I guess the closest thing would be to imagine a great tragedy, seeing an earthquake or tornado on TV in a town your family lives in. You don't hear anything from them for hours until finally you get through. They are all right, it's missed them. That's how it felt; my underdeveloped and overly dramatic view of the world, never really having confronted tragedy. At least not yet...

Later that night I'd gotten ready for bed and was contemplating rubbing one out after such a close release, when my phone vibrated.

> HER
>
> If you aren't sleeping yet, I'm ready...

I was dumbfounded. She couldn't mean ready for it, could she?

> ?

> Come to my house? My parents are sleeping.

Needless to say, I went, sneaking in the sliding glass doors off the kitchen as she pulled me by my hand, stifling a giggle. My body was on fire, my limbs tingling. There was no hesitation this time as we removed every article of clothing, taking each other in with the shedding of each layer, consuming one another. I can still remember the feel of her, the goosebumps. My toes cracking as I came, and the mint on her breath.

We became us.

I JUMPED as a car door slammed outside, and I ran to the window, toppling a chair in the process. Our neighbor was struggling to balance grocery bags as their oldest child stood off to the side, playing on his phone. So it wasn't her.

"Come on."

The adrenaline coursed through me as I opened and closed my hands. They'd grown tingly with my anxiety, and no matter how much I moved, I couldn't seem to settle, my stomach churning to the point I thought I would shit. It felt like my body was breaking down.

Where was she? The scars inside me were tearing open, raw as if new, pain bubbling to the surface. How could she? It was just like then, like before.

We'd been dating for eleven months when I decided the time was right for her to be my wife. I couldn't imagine my life moving forward without her being a part of it.

Everyone told me we were too young. Her parents looked at me skeptically when I asked for their blessing, their reluctant agreement making me wonder if I was doing the right thing. But I needed her. My short twenty-three years had never been better. I had so much to learn.

We'd taken the train to the city, a day of shopping and exploring planned, with a trip to the planetarium to indulge my nerdy tendencies for space. She huffed at the last but said *fine,* since I'd wanted to do it. She didn't know what else I had in store for us.

The day was beautiful and sunny, with perfect temperatures and a light breeze off the lake. I was in my own world, on cloud nine. I was blissfully and intentionally ignorant.

Throughout the day she'd seemed removed; there, but not. I showered her with intimate touches and exclamations of my love, only to be met with lukewarm responses. I'd thought it wasn't her day; she was just off. She didn't know why I put together a packed day, so I couldn't expect her to be as jubilant as I was. Nevertheless, it nagged at me, which I buried beneath layers of optimism.

We got to the planetarium, and the ticket agent shared a conspiratorial smirk with me as he told us our seat numbers. The room was dark and filled with patrons, an artificial vista of the sky above the city on the domed ceiling above. I clutched her hand tightly, and she kept trying to escape my grip, complaining that my hand was too sweaty.

Minutes went by, and I held my breath. The show was a blur as I struggled to contain myself, waiting for it to end. And then it did.

The ceiling went black, and a few stars blinked back to life, quieting the restless crowd, who thought it was over. The stars began to move, coalescing directly above our seats, and we could hear the whispers as the anticipation built.

I turned to her, my other hand coming out of my pocket. The phrase "Will You Marry Me?" formed like a constellation across the domed sky, and my eyes met hers as if on cue. She looked back at me, wide-eyed, like a deer caught in headlights.

I'd done it. I'd surprised her. I opened the box, the solitaire gleaming within.

"Will you?"

Gasps and hushed exclamations sounded all around, and, in the faint light, I could see her wilting, folding in on herself to hide from the crowd.

I finally allowed myself to take in our setting, sensing my mistake. She abhorred having the spotlight on her. How could I have been so stupid?

I took a deep, cleansing breath. It could still be salvaged. She just needed to say yes so we could flee, begin our life together, and joke about this public spectacle from the privacy of our own space.

"What did she say?" somebody yelled.

Her eyes were still on mine, panicked. My stomach roiled.

"Will you?" I asked again, my tone higher pitched than I'd wanted.

She nodded and mouthed *yeah,* her wide eyes never leaving mine. I slid the ring on her finger.

"She said yes!" I shouted, and the whole theater cheered, my ass and back sweating profusely.

I grabbed her hand, and we fled as quickly as possible, as I knew that was what she wanted. Congratulations and cheers followed us, and I waved behind me like a politician leaving the stage. Her eyes were still wide.

"Surprise," I'd said, trying to take the edge off.

"Yeah, surprise..."

"It's what you want, right?"

She cleared her throat. "I said yes."

"Okay," I said cheerfully, overcompensating for what she wasn't giving me.

We rode home in silence.

That summer became the first trial of our relationship. We hardly saw each other for the first two months of our engagement.

"I just need time to think and see my friends."

"About us?" I'd asked, confused.

"Just about everything."

She wouldn't look at me while we talked.

"Do you not want to marry me?"

That brought eye contact and anger.

"I already said yes, okay. I just want some time."

Two months. Two months of the same conversation. Two months of the same questions and answers. Two months of questioning my choices and my self-worth. She wouldn't talk to me, like really talk to me. I had no idea what I'd done or what she was grappling with. I couldn't eat or sleep, replaying our whole relationship repeatedly in my head, searching for why she'd say yes and immediately pull away.

Until one day, she'd called and asked to come over. It was like it never happened. She wanted to be us again, move in together, and begin wedding planning.

I asked if everything was okay and what had happened, but she told me nothing and said she just needed a fun summer before becoming a married woman. She stated it with joy and casualness, ignoring the hurt she'd seen on my face every time I tried to talk to her, or the phone calls that ended with me in tears.

"Was there someone else?" I dared to ask, fearing the answer so much I had to get drunk before asking her.

"No, of course not," she told me, but her eye contact was off-kilter. There was the tell, a shift to her eyes.

"You promise?"

She laughed and grabbed my face in her hands, kissing me. "Of course."

She'd said it with her eyes closed. I should have known then—I did know then, but like her, I just shut my eyes.

I OPENED my phone and looked at the pictures I'd saved, the heat rising in my cheeks to the point of pain. My eyes were open, and I was finally looking. I'm not sure what led me to suspect, to dig deeper. Perhaps it was the more frequent downturn of her eyes when we locked gazes, just like before, but I buried it like a fool. It was always there festering, the noxious waste in the sewer just below the surface, absorbing everything I poured down my metaphorical drain until, at last, the shit overflowed, desecrating the streets.

I thought we may even have gotten past any low place—that is, until the second trial of our relationship, which reared its head last year.

We'd finally started looking at homes. That'd been impossible the first several years of our marriage, as I was laid off and struggling to find work, the Great Recession of 2008 in full force, crippling a whole generation that was promised the stars in the '90s if they just went to college. What a load of shit.

Those years were tough, but they were like the ones before our engagement; we seemed in love, even though not always happy, with fights breaking out monthly over bills and money. She wanted to shop, have dinner dates, and buy new furniture, but we couldn't afford it; for part of that time, we even had to move in with my parents.

I tried to sacrifice by not buying myself new clothes for almost three consecutive years so that she could do what she pleased, trying to let her have some normalcy. Then the recession eased, and I finally got a well-paying finance job. The next couple of years got better. I was still tight with money, like survivors of the Depression era, not entirely trusting the system to hold, but we saved for our first home and were finally ready.

The day we'd signed our mortgage papers, she realized her period was late. I knew how it happened. Celebrations for my birthday had led us to throw caution to the wind. We were married, and children were part of the plan. So just like that, two lines appeared on the plastic stick; not the kind you had to read between—we both knew what they meant.

A few weeks later, the doctor verified it for us, and we eagerly absorbed this new part of our lives into our plans. We'd have a baby, and I'd be a dad. The idea didn't hit home until I heard the heartbeat, proof of our combined union. I fell in love again, my heart expanding to embrace this embodiment of us, half her and half me.

One night around the thirteen-week mark, I went to the grocery store, leaving her home alone for an hour. While in the checkout line, an unfamiliar number appeared on my phone. It was the hospital. She'd tripped on the stairs.

When I arrived at her room, the doctor broke the news. That new piece of my heart, the life we'd made, was gone. She wouldn't speak to me or anyone else. No matter how hard I tried to be there for her, to love, to mourn, she pulled back, her eyes perpetually downcast. I spent my days and nights numbly, going so far as to cry to my mother, since my wife wouldn't respond, at the loss of what could have been.

I gave her space, and a pall of sorrow, thick as wildfire smoke, shrouded our home, smothering the light that once shone there.

At night, I'd reach for her, but she'd flinch at my touch, resulting in me curling in upon myself, my appendages shriveling like a poisoned spider in its death throes. We went about the motions of life, but it was a farce that everyone saw through. Yet time heals all wounds, or so they say.

After several months, her shroud lifted, and it was almost like when that first flower bud peaked through the snow in early spring, prefacing a time of renewal and rebirth. We started to go on dates and make love again. It felt like nothing after that could ruin us if our loss hadn't.

We saw friends, and she often went out with just the girls, catching up after the great pause in her life. I was grateful she was back.

It didn't take long for the late nights to begin, though. On more than one occasion, she came home stumbling and struggling to make it up the stairs to our bedroom, but I held my tongue, knowing that despite our lives moving forward, her grief was still very much present. We didn't talk about it, and once again, I shut my eyes.

I WIPED my hand across my cheeks, the tears cool on my skin. After everything we'd been through, how could she? It didn't matter anymore. I had my proof.

I grabbed the dining room chair and placed it near the front window, just to the side of the curtain. I had to remain on watch. I needed to confront her right when she got home, before my resolve had time to break.

That whole time, I'd thought she was grieving, and it turned out I was just a naive fool. When she began to cool to me yet again, I made excuses for her. But when someone grieves, do they develop shifty eyes, looking away at the least distraction? It got to the point where I felt she sought them so she didn't have to make eye contact.

How about flinching? It was hardly perceptible, akin to a shiver brought on by a draft, and anytime I mentioned it, the reasonable response was given with a smile: "I'm just cold." But after my every touch?

I tried to tell myself that it was nothing, I was overreacting; but I couldn't shake the sense that something was there, my fears clawing to the surface.

I never wanted to become one of those partners who broke the privacy barrier, but after months of frigidness between us, I needed to know the truth. Something was amiss, and I finally needed to open my eyes to our reality. I checked her text messages on her iPad when she wasn't home, knowing her account synced across her devices.

What I found was not what I expected. I thought maybe I was just being paranoid and I'd find nothing, or perhaps text messages to her friends indicating that I'd done something obscure that set her off. Had I been insensitive about how she was still handling losing the baby? No, that wasn't it.

Instead, I found suggestions and descriptive actions. I found reminiscences of times before, a summer of fun to send her off. And I found pictures, a cock, and fellatio that had nothing to do with me, a photo record immortalizing my ultimate fear.

I fell to my knees in our bedroom as I looked at each incriminating image, wondering what I had done wrong or what I could have done differently to prevent this. Why hadn't our love been enough?

I'd snapped photos of it all on my own phone, knowing I'd need to confront her and, without this reminder, this tangible log, I'd allow myself to be coaxed back from the ledge.

FINALLY, I heard a car door shut outside the house, and the sound carried through the window screen. I knew instinctually, it was her. I felt the hair on my neck rise like a cat poised to pounce. My wife was near. Was I ready for this?

My leg started to bounce, moving involuntarily while my stomach constricted into a hard ball of denial and dread.

I can't do this.

The door opened, and I froze, that familiar sense of wholeness filling me, her beauty constricting my breath. I couldn't do it. I needed her. But why didn't she need me?

She set her purse down on the kitchen counter, balancing with her palm as she leaned over to remove one of her heels, the underside scuffed and worn as much as her purse. That can't be right. She was always so meticulous about how she looked.

I stepped into the kitchen, and she looked over at me, dropping her other heel to the floor and smiling at me.

That warm, beautiful smile, but behind it, hidden in its depths, was the secret, the insidious daemon that lessened her dimples just enough for me to see its fraudulence. Our eyes met, and she froze, her eyes drifting ever so slightly so as not to hold my gaze.

"I...," I said, trailing off as I felt my voice catch. I cleared my throat, knowing it must be said, and stood straighter; her posture matched mine.

"We need to talk."

Her smile vanished, the edges of her lips lowering into a line, and another crack appeared; her lipstick slightly smeared at the edges of her mouth.

"What's wrong, honey? Talk about what?" she asked.

There was a tremor in her voice, stripping her naked before me. The anxiety was like a bullhorn in my ears, widening the chasm between us.

"I—I saw the messages... and the photos. I know about..."

I couldn't say more. I didn't need to. Her eyes betrayed her, those beautiful blue pools filling with tears.

Without a rebuttal, she'd confirmed it; there was nothing to say. Her mouth started to move, but all I could hear was the muffled noise of my world crumbling around me.

She stepped toward me and hesitated as I raised my hand, looking away. I couldn't face her; everything she had been suddenly became a mockery of what I thought I'd known about who she was. It was like I wasn't even in my own body anymore, just a casual observer of this horrific scene of heartbreak.

Time seemed to shift in a dark haze of sorrow and regrets.

Dazed, I turned away from her and headed for the back door, leaving the house lest I collapse beneath the rubble of our marriage. Everything had ended: my perfect life, my perfect love. It was all gone, even though only a fool would believe it had ever been there to begin with.

The door slammed behind me, and I hesitated momentarily to see if she would follow, my resolve wavering. She wasn't there, the kitchen window empty of all life, a visualization of our love on display.

"I'm sorry... we're through," I whispered, wishing I could have said the words my leaving conveyed, but I couldn't. No matter how dark my life was, our illusion had been my brightest moment, and now everything was gone. I had nothing left. Like the great void in space after a supernova, I was empty.

Bowing my head, I walked away from the house as it started to drizzle, accepting my place in the apparent cliché as the heartbroken man stuck in the rain; the divine comedy of our first date.

With my head hung, I continued into the night, never to return and never looking back. My world was before me, my eyes wide open, and there was only darkness.

PHANTOM IN THE VOID

J ust as she'd done for over fifty years, Laverne closed her fingers
around her husband's hand. Their daughter sat across from
her, face framed by blonde hair, looking down on the man who
stood as her beacon her entire life, her strength. The generations
circled the bed, whimpers and sobs permeating as they watched the
decay of their patriarch. He was Grandpa and, for some, Dad. But for
her, he was always Buck.

She felt a squeeze, and goosebumps flourished on her arm. *He
knows I'm here*, she thought before he sucked in some air. A curdling
rattle escaped his lips as he exhaled. She shivered and felt another
piece of herself fall away.

"Buck..."

Her vision blurred, the room becoming an indiscernible swath of
pink through the salty tears. He'd always strived to make her happy,
even acquiescing when she wanted to decorate their bedroom in
those gendered hues, not caring other than being with her. All her
stubbornness... for what? What she wouldn't give for one more day.
All the demands she would take back...

The chaplain placed his hand on her shoulder. She nodded, not facing him, knowing what he intended. He spoke the words—the final prayer, that goodbye neither Laverne nor their descendants had the strength to give. His words hung in the air, a blanket of faith to insulate them from the raw pain. Laverne reached for it, grasping in the dark, lost in a haze of sorrow and numbness.

"Is there anything you want to say to him?"

Laverne knew what she had to say, but she choked back the words. She covered her face with her hands, trying to hold the tears back by force. How could she do it? Once she said it, she could never take it back. She'd be branding her soul with an indelible mark.

She looked up and saw her daughter watching her, tears glistening on her splotchy cheeks. Her daughter's piercing blue eyes stayed even as she nodded her approval, as if to say, "Go ahead, Mom."

"Let go, Buck..."

Laverne's voice was steady, even as her body trembled, tears streaming unfelt from her eyes. It was like she wasn't in her body.

She inhaled a shaky breath and looked at the chaplain.

"That's his nickname," she said, voice hoarse.

He looked back at her with a pitying smile, not condescending, but an acknowledgment of a loss he didn't envy. A series of short, mournful laughs bounced around the room; sniffles mixed with hiccups as everyone felt that momentary reprieve from their grief.

Laverne looked at her husband, his mouth open and face wan as the candle of life within him flickered. She stood and bent to kiss him one last time.

"Buck? It's okay... let go," she whispered, lips still caressing his cheek. He sucked in another breath and, as if her words were the turn of a key, he finally listened; anything for her.

He exhaled.

Buck's final breath of life escaped his lips, signifying that last moment, that goodbye he so desperately would have wanted to say.

Laverne couldn't move, nobody could.

She stared at her husband, her foundation and pillar, a single tear rolling down his cheek, reflecting her empty world back at her. Her family ceased to exist at that moment. It was just her and Buck, his breath dispersing around the room, diffusing his life to extinction.

"No...," she choked out, feeling her legs shake. What had she done?

If she moved quickly, she could breathe him in. She could take that last breath into herself, suck it right out of the air into her lungs, just for her. He couldn't go.

"No, no, no, no, no."

She lunged at the bed, her hands grasping for something unseen, flailing.

"No!"

Her single exclamation grew in its speed and ferocity. She took it back: it wasn't okay. He needed to come back.

She crawled across the bed, breathing heavily, trying desperately to inhale as much air as possible, but her shouts and mournful gasps prevented her from doing so.

"Mom."

Her daughter's voice floated somewhere off in the distance, muted by Laverne's shock and lightheadedness.

She took in one final gulp, and she knew then that he was gone. All that effort was for naught; she couldn't grab hold of him. The emptiness was glaring.

Her grandkids were all moving toward her, reality in slow motion. They were all there to be with her and support her, but she only wanted him—her Buck.

She wanted to keep holding her breath, afraid to release whatever part of him she could capture, but instinct won out in the end. Her exhalation was a whoosh of sound followed by immeasurable fatigue as clamps of flesh engulfed her arms to prevent her from falling.

Laverne opened her mouth to protest, demanding to be left to go with Buck, but words didn't escape her lips. Laverne didn't hold back, her cry drowning out the world. A wail, akin to the sorrow one could only imagine was felt throughout the ages by every widow who had lost their love, overpowered the sobs and murmurs of worry.

Her strength evaporated, and she crumpled, her deadweight

pulling her grandchildren to the ground with her. The pain took on a physical presence, a hole ripping through her heart. Laverne's daughter helped her to a chair.

Slumped over, she saw the chaplain, solemn in the presence of the family's grief, step toward Buck and try to close his eyes. They kept springing open.

"They don't seem to want to stay closed."

Laverne looked at her husband, her family's combined embrace acting as a wall that kept her from him. Resigned to her fate, she didn't fight it, desperately trying to find warmth in her cold abyss.

"You're always so damn hard-headed," she yelled at him, wishing he would respond. A chuckle. An "Oh, shit" like he used to. Anything. But all she heard was the sniffling and breathing of her family.

"Buck..."

Fog crept in from the window across the room, and Laverne let it take her until she realized she couldn't see him anymore.

"Buck? Buck?"

Each time she called his name, the note of hysteria increased. Her words echoed back as though in a vast chamber of emptiness. Everyone was gone.

"Buck?"

A hand grabbed her arm. She couldn't see it but felt its pressure, intensifying and moving her through the darkness.

"Buck?"

———

LAVERNE'S EYES OPENED, blinking away tears.

A woman stood near her bed, looking down at her, forehead scrunched and blue eyes, framed with blonde hair, shimmering. She looked familiar, but Laverne couldn't place her. She wiped her eyes, not remembering why she would have been crying.

"Mom, wake up. Are you okay?"

Who is she talking to? Where am I?

Laverne looked away from the woman toward the window. Two armchairs were placed on either side of a table with a lamp, the chair on the left occupied by a pillow shaped like a golf ball with the letters B-U-C-K stitched across it. Something about that word tugged at her, the pink walls of her room glowing in the afternoon sun.

Why are there two chairs? Buck... who was... WAIT!

"Mom?" the blonde woman said, a worried edge to her tone.

The connection snapped, fleeting as quickly as light once the filaments in a bulb separated, leaving behind its blackened shell.

Her head whirled back to the blonde woman.

"I almost had it. You ruined it!"

The woman flinched as if slapped, and the look on her face matched the action. Laverne looked away, banishing any feelings of remorse for the pain she'd caused. This woman had no right.

"Just let me sleep."

The woman sighed, and Laverne could hear the sound of swishing fabric as the woman's pants rubbed against her duvet.

"I'll be in the other room if you need me."

The woman started to close the door and then stopped.

"And, Mom?"

"Yes?" Laverne asked.

"I love you."

The words stabbed like a knife in her heart, clearing her mind like a ray of light peeking through a cloud. *It is her.*

"I love you too, Cheryl."

The door closed, and Laverne could hear the distant sound of sorrow. She wasn't sure why her daughter would cry; maybe they both lived in a perpetual state of murky darkness, the sun only illuminating what once was on the rarest occasion.

Her eyes drifted back to the pillow in the chair.

"Buck..."

Tears flowed, but they were untethered, devoid of the specific anchor that would give gravity to what she was losing.

Closing her eyes, a light sparkled in the darkness. Laverne

reached for it, but it was fleeting, stretching farther and farther away the harder she tried to get it. She struggled, swimming against the current of the abyss, until the light winked out, leaving her alone in the void, groping in the dark for the lost love she no longer remembered.

Buck...

ECHOES

Katelyn's hands trembled again, and she squeezed them together, frowning at their involuntary movement. It kept happening. Was she sick again?

She told everyone that she had a weird illness, but really, it was the need that got to her—treatment for a simple slipped disc that turned into an endless craving, a constant need for more.

"Mom?"

"What, Jay? I'm in my room."

"Can I come in?"

"No! Look... I'm tired, okay?" She grabbed several pill bottles from her nightstand and felt a pang of dread from the silence. She'd trained herself to listen for the sweet sound of the pills rattling, signaling that the pain would subside soon, if only for a while. Not this time.

She slid the empty bottles under her bed, her jaw clenching. She couldn't get her mind off of how much it hurt.

"I'm hungry."

"I just bought something to eat. Check the fridge."

"I did... Ugh, forget it." His voice trailed off. A slam of a door announced his retreat to his room. Her sweet little boy had become a young man. What had happened to him?

Fuck it hurts.

Clenching harder, she got out of bed and moved to her door. She hesitated at the knob, her fingers mere inches from the outside realities she locked herself away from. Could she face the world right now? Her uncertain reality?

The sickness had lasted for months, and the decline was quickening. Being a recluse was the best course for everyone. Several friends came over and tried speaking with her, but she wasn't up to it. Nobody needed to see her like this. She knew she needed to make a stronger effort, but after missing her last shift and getting fired, she couldn't overcome her insecurity.

Jesus, Katelyn, it's just the living room.

She turned the knob.

Her kitchen was dark, and half the light bulbs overhead were missing from their sockets because she couldn't afford to replace them. Lights were a luxury item, along with facial tissue and napkins. They'd make do.

What was Jay talking about? There is a package of cheese right here.

She pulled it from the refrigerator and took a slice out of the plastic sleeve. Flinching, she dropped the moldy cheese to the floor.

I just bought this!

Her jaw twitched, and she ground her teeth together.

"Mom, what are you doing?"

"What the hell happened to the cheese I just bought?"

"That's all that has been in there for two weeks."

He lowered his eyes and shrunk into himself as she glared at him.

"No, I just bought it! This refrigerator's empty. Where is everything I just got?"

Her stomach lurched, and reality returned as the rumble of his stomach echoed throughout the kitchen. Jay rested his hands on his belly.

"Oh buddy, I... I'm sorry. I don't feel well—"

"Can you take me back to Dad's?"

"No! Why?"

Jay's brow furrowed as his eyes met hers. "I'm hungry... and I want somebody to talk to. You're always in your room."

"What? No, I'm just tired. Let's go to Subway. No problem!" Her voice was high-pitched and frantic.

I need it.

She opened her bathroom cabinet and found one last pill hidden in the top of her shaving cream can, between the lid and the dispenser. Just to take the edge off. It went down roughly as her cotton mouth worked against her.

I can sell the TV tomorrow; we don't need two. Then, some food and a refill. Just a little more... It will all be okay.

"Jay. Let's go, buddy."

She heard nothing.

"Jay?"

His room seemed cold, as if he hadn't been there for weeks. The light switch did nothing to activate the bulb-less lamps. Where was he?

She pulled on a sweater and huffed on her hands. Sixty-four degrees? She cranked the thermostat up, but nothing happened.

"Jay?"

A faint glow from the coffee table caught her eye—a text message on her phone.

> **BRYAN**
>
> This was your last chance. I'm not letting him go through this shit anymore. Custody's mine. I thought you were a better mom than this. You better never lecture me again.

She collapsed to her knees. Tears flowed like a burst dam as the haze cleared. The custody battle, the injury at work, the hunger, the shame, the judgment... the pain.

God, the pain...

She itched a raw patch on her wrist before swiping the tears on her face with her sleeve. Her fingertips were bloody.

"I need just a little more... then it will all be okay."

She tore apart her room, looking for one more pill, just a little something to get her through. Clothes were flung into the air, and she drove a knife into her mattress, convinced she had once hidden something in there.

Her hands trembled more violently than before, the quaking moving up her arms like a ripple in the water once the tossed stone made contact. Her teeth chattered, shattering the silence that could only be filled with her thoughts.

"I need help," she whispered, an admission she had fought so hard to make.

Katelyn's father had warned her when she got pregnant at nineteen that the "charity bus" was over, and throughout the years, he'd held to that declaration. The first time she'd lost a job and couldn't make rent, he'd simply told her, "Well, I hope you figure it out; my grandson needs somewhere to sleep."

She eventually found a solution, knowing she couldn't rely on the inconsistency of her relationship with Bryan, let alone his employment status. Her whole life became an act of doing things in spite of her childhood authority figures.

But she may finally be broken enough to beg... for Jay.

Katelyn shivered and looked around her living room, her raw, exposed fingertips the only part of her visible. She remembered being in her room, not on her couch, and, in a daze, she stepped over the pile of crusted vomit on the carpet to peek through the curtains. Everything was white.

"Snow?"

That couldn't be right; Bryan's text came right after Jay's birthday in September. She needed her phone.

She floated through her home as she searched, a noiseless phantom haunting her halls. Her pain was finally gone, but she felt too light and so very cold.

"Damn," she said, dropping her phone onto the bedside table. Its battery was dead and the electricity was off, so she couldn't charge it. She'd sworn she'd gone for help, to do what she needed for Jay. She had really meant to. If only she could call him and let him know... No, she needed to go to him.

Katelyn gathered her resolve and walked to the bathroom to get ready.

"No."

Her voice was quiet despite the shock, but a part of her knew this was true. The eviction notice dated December 15 was open on the counter next to an empty bottle of pills.

She gazed in the mirror. Her robed body lay at her feet, eyes blank, vomit caked to her chin and shirt. Kneeling, she began to shake her corpse as the memories came back to her. She'd tried to get clean, reaching out to friends who desperately tried to be there for her. They'd taken her to appointments and addiction meetings, helped her get groceries, and spotted her enough cash to keep the lights on.

She'd been on her way back to her boy for almost two months, knowing she'd owe her friends for the food and the money, but certain that asking for help was the right thing. She hadn't figured out how to pay rent—or at least how to do it and still build up an emergency supply of the pills. The pain had waned, but she worried what she'd do if it came back, and she couldn't afford to buy the pills later. She'd still had time; she could do this.

Katelyn had called Jay, and Bryan answered his phone. He'd told her that if she kept cleaning up her act, he'd consider letting her see Jay, but she needed to prove it to them. Thanksgiving was approaching, and Bryan finally consented to bring Jay by and, while unimpressed with the conditions of the house, he'd thought she seemed better.

"You look like you again."

She'd smiled at him despite not wanting the compliment, but being acknowledged for her hard work felt good.

"Thanks. I really am trying, Bryan."

Then his eyes had narrowed. He was looking past her right shoulder. Jay was standing there, holding her emergency bottle of pills.

Bryan hadn't bothered to say a word, grabbing Jay by the hand

and storming out despite her protests and explanations. The pain had come rushing back then, and time escaped her as she chewed her fingers and scratched her skin raw, trying to force it away.

The eviction notice had arrived with a knock three days later.

Katelyn returned to herself with a sharp inhalation of breath and jumped to her feet. She gave her body a hard shove with her foot, her fury boiling over.

"We were almost us again! Why couldn't you just be strong for him? Why?"

She kicked at her body again and again, but the corpse moved no more than the leaves of a tree on a still day. She was nothing more than a shadow of herself as the pieces of memory became whole.

She'd never get to say goodbye or tell Jay how proud she was to be his mother. Her baby would grow up haunted by the false demons that he wasn't enough to save her or maybe that she didn't love him. She had been a mere echo of what she should have been for him, and the reverberations of her life would now still into nothing more than a memory of what could have been.

Her hands trembled no more.

THE GRAVE SPOTTER

How chill the wind was on the day of a funeral, how sorrowful the rain. It was a hard week; my wife, my heart, who was talking to me just seventy-two short hours prior, was now being buried. These moments make me question the point of seeking out a loved one just to see them leave you in any number of ways. I'd had ample warning of what life could throw at me when my mother died from a grueling battle with cancer when I was only eight; but, like most of humanity, I must get some sick pleasure out of suffering.

I swore I would keep my distance, but I didn't listen. She came into my life unexpectedly, and I fell for her in an instant; our life together was like a tragic skydiving accident, gravity pulling us down until that horrible point where my parachute worked, and hers did not, separating us forever with her untimely impact.

God, I miss her. Mom would have liked her...

The funeral came together rather suddenly; I didn't even have a black suit, just an old brown one that hardly fit me with a slight tear on the elbow.

"I need a suit. I can't wear this one," I'd said, hands flailing about as my best friend, Dan, looked on.

"Trev, it's okay. She won't mind."

"It matters!" I said, rounding on him.

I felt weak and faint, and arms encircled me before I collapsed.

"It does, buddy. Just don't worry about that part. I'll get you a suit."

I held his arms around me, a moment of intimate touch that I'd needed then to make sure I didn't plummet into the darkness forever.

Finally, I let out a small laugh as I choked back tears.

"It can be rented. Just make sure nothing is frayed. She wouldn't want me to look like that."

"Shhh, I know, buddy, I know."

I shuddered at the memory of how broken I was yesterday. With so many tears and obsessions, I couldn't just stick to the matter at hand. Not when the matter at hand was my wife's funeral.

Rough fabric rubbed against my neck as I adjusted my tie in the mirror. It was all black, the way it should be. If only the collar had been a bit less starched.

"Are you ready?" I asked my reflection in the mirror.

I exhaled.

The rain was persistent, but I didn't hurry or avoid it as I stepped out of the house onto the cold street of my neighborhood and the cool drops splashed against me, the water spots hidden by my suit's dark hue.

I stood in front of the home we shared together and I watched as cars drove by at regular intervals, tires splashing in the puddles rhythmically like the beat of my heart. If they stopped, would I do the same?

A red blob pulled in front of me like a smear of blood; the raindrops accumulated in my eyelashes, blurring my vision.

"Trev, get in. You look soaked."

I wiped my eyes with the back of my hand, and a red BMW, Breana's car, coalesced.

I got into the backseat, shoulders slumped, reluctant to be the widowed passenger in need of a chauffeur. It seemed silly, but I knew

I was in no condition to drive myself. Hell, I didn't know if I'd ever be able to drive again. Not after the accident.

"Are you okay back there? I can turn the heat up," Bre said, her eyes fixed on me in the rearview mirror.

"No, it's alright."

The world moved around me, vertigo teaming up with the car's movement. As if what I was about to face wasn't enough of a trial, my car sickness had to rear its ugly head. Maybe I should have sat in the front seat.

I slumped down further, letting my body slide to my right until my cheek rested on the cool leather, putting Bre's face in profile. And just like that, she was there: my wife, my Monaciel. I knew intellectually that her sister was driving, but the dagger to my heart was no less sharp or precise.

I clenched my eyes shut, squeezing out the tears like juice from a lemon.

Mona was everywhere. I didn't want her to go, yet I couldn't endure the continuous reminders.

Opening my eyes again, she was still there, the features distinctly Bre's but with Mona's ghost. The curve of her nose. The Cindy Crawford beauty mark above her lip. The way she gently moved a flyaway piece of her hair and positioned it behind her ear.

"Mona..."

"Hmm?" Bre intoned, her gray eyes looking back at me in the rearview mirror again; same color but a different shape, and despite that, I could see Mona superimposed over Bre, like trying to look at a 3D image without the special glasses.

"I think I'm going to be sick."

"Oh shit, not in the car!"

Bre slammed on the brakes and pulled off the road, jarring me back to reality as I pushed open the car door and released a mouthful of bile. The acidity scorched my throat, a cleansing.

"Trev, are you okay?" she asked as she fussed with her seatbelt.

I waved my hand over my head, praying she would take the cue to calm down and stay in the car; nobody needed to see this. I was sure she could already smell it.

"Just a tissue, please."

She handed me one along with a sanitizing wipe, and I swabbed my mouth and fingers, both covered in sticky digestive fluid.

"Take your time, it's okay."

How could Bre be this strong for me? I wasn't the only one who lost somebody in that accident. In the blink of an eye, she'd lost her sister and best friend. I remember making that call to let Bre know what had happened. I hadn't been able to get the words out on the phone, but after a few moments of me weeping, Bre knew. Her screams are just as vivid in my memory as my own.

I closed the door, thankful that the rain had stopped so I didn't arrive at the funeral home drenched and looking even more of a mess than I already was. I splayed my body across the backseat; I didn't have the strength to sit up.

"You can go," I whispered.

Bre nodded and faced forward. In that brief moment, when we made eye contact, I saw the strain, the struggle to continue her posture of strength.

"Bre—"

"Just a few more minutes, and we'll be there," she said, cutting me short as she began to drive.

I shut my eyes and let myself float away.

———

WHEN I ENTERED the funeral home, Bre beside me, conversation buzzed around us, but I couldn't home in on anything. I had become the living dead, my body moving but my mind sedentary. Familiar faces furrowed with concern as I passed, tissues dabbing their raccooned eyes—the sniffles of mourning punctuating the sorrowful ambience.

I didn't want to be there, all eyes on me as I took my long march to the casket, forcing me to burrow ever further into my shell of isolation.

When would this horrible nightmare end? When would a final jump-scare make me flinch enough to wake in my bed, Mona curled beside me, still breathing and intact? She had to be alive still, or it meant there truly was no higher power looking out for me. I wanted to scream.

"Look at her," Bre said, voice clipped, eyes shining with welled tears.

I looked at the photo collage next to Mona's casket. Her smile was everywhere, intermixed with my own, her bright gray eyes shining like a ray of light in my darkness. My fingers brushed her face, but it was flat, lifeless. Just a photo. Oh, Monaciel... my beloved Mona.

Azaleas covered every open space around her casket in a variety of vases. Mona hadn't liked them, but I let her family arrange everything seeing as I couldn't even look at her body after she died—Bre had to identify her—let alone figure out how to get a suit for myself. It seems as though Bre lost the flower battle with her mother.

"There he is," Mona's father, John Pierre, said, hand outstretched and composed. His face was dry, not a sign of puffiness, as if he hadn't just lost his daughter. And, of course, his suit looked tailored; his outward appearance was always the most crucial thing to him. The guy was morally bankrupt: he cheated on the mother of his children and abandoned Mona and Bre when they were just thirteen and eleven for a woman half his age. Yet the sisters had agreed to see him again when he reached out more than a decade later, reconnecting with their long-lost father. Mona was the saint I never could be.

I felt my face redden. I was getting hot. This couldn't be real... I couldn't do this—deal with her father without her.

I needed her to be the intermediary. I always had, with John having told me I wasn't good enough for her the first time I'd met him. That was rich coming from him.

I began to sway on my feet, taking a step backward, fluttering my eyes, trying to clear my vision. I needed to escape.

"John, I can't..."

A hand touched my shoulder, giving me a comforting squeeze and steadying me on my feet.

"Trev, do you need anything?"

Dan. Bless him.

"Mr. Pierre, good to see you again," Dan said, extending his hand to shake John's.

John pursed his lips like he'd eaten something sour and harrumphed before turning to greet mourners approaching the casket, leaving Dan with his hand outstretched. The man loved his spotlight.

Dan shrugged, placed his hand on my lower back, and guided me to stand behind the collage on its easel, giving me the most minuscule, yet highly desired, shred of privacy.

"The second I saw him, I knew you'd need an assist."

I nodded and sighed.

"I've rarely dealt with him without her. Every time I see him, I want to hit him."

"Probably not a good idea at a funeral," Dan said, his lip curling up on one side. I get finding amusement when it comes, I just didn't know if he realized how serious I was.

A line of people formed just to the left of me, and I could see Bre watching Dan and me through the rows of flowers in their tall vases that lined the path to the coffin, her eyes shifting to us and then back to the parade of people giving her their condolences. Eyeing the onlookers, I could see they were trying hard not to look at me and whispering to each other.

I cleared my throat. Dan grabbed my shoulders.

"Look, I know it's hard, but you only have a few more steps. You don't have to stand right next to the casket if you don't want to, but there are a lot of people who want to pay their respects to both her and you," Dan said, gesturing over his shoulder toward Mona's family. "They need you."

I shook my head; my mind clouded with flashbacks of an endless parade of hugs and kisses from faceless acquaintances after my mom passed. That had shattered me—Mom was the only parent I'd ever known.

My grandparents had taken me to what seemed like an endless number of therapists, and nothing broke through. I was failing at school and near the point of being held back a year when we started studying jazz in music class. The sounds of the brass became distinctly mine and acted as a siren song to lead me back to the land of the living. It was as if the notes connected right to my soul.

Mona and I bonded over it. We met in a jazz club, and her proficiency with the saxophone was just a drop in the bucket of all the things I loved about her. It became a hallmark of us. A night on the town almost always led to a jazz club. A ride in our car or having cocktails at our home resulted in jazz playing loudly as we vibed to the sounds. We were old souls who felt we belonged in a bygone era musically, and I could no longer hear any of my favorites without thinking of her; it linked us. Then the car accident happened.

That magic that connected us for so many years, those notes and sounds that helped me when I was young, back from the brink of despair due to my mother's death, overnight became a gateway to a chasm of darkness I may never recover from.

Fly me away... the opening lyrics to our favorite song by Gigi McLean started playing in my head, and I started to shake.

"I can't," I whispered.

Dan squeezed my shoulders and nodded, pulling me out of my reverie. His face was defeated, eyes sunken pits, but the twinkle they held conveyed hope.

"You have to," he whispered back.

Time seemed to stand still or move in fast forward; I'm not sure which. All I could discern were blurry columns of black-clad figures lined up for as long as my tear-impaired eyes could see as Dan moved me into position.

My lugubrious expression was met with sympathetic shakes of the head or an occasional mournful hug, but none of it mattered. I was alone despite Mona's family on either side of me. No amount of sympathy would bring her back; nothing would stop that drunk asshole from slamming into her or bring me the justice I deserved. He should be in this box, not her. Not my Monaciel...

I risked a look at her to see her face one last time, but my cheeks began to tingle and saliva pooled in my mouth—a precursor to another bout of bile ejection—as my eyes traced the long lines of the gunmetal casket, her six-thousand-dollar escape pod from this life.

"I need some air," I shouted and pushed my way through the remaining spectators to this tragedy, a series of grunts and looks of affront following my blitz to the hall.

I fell to my knees once I made it to the entryway as the heavy aroma of frankincense, myrrh, and mothballs danced a violent jig in my nostrils. I couldn't get enough air, and each inhalation intensified my inability to breathe.

I needed to let it out. The pain and fear, and, my God, the grief. I opened my mouth to yell, to expel it all, but the bile came up instead. It hadn't been enough to actually vomit, but it scorched my throat and stopped any future attempts at screaming.

"Shit," I croaked between tears and heaves.

"Trev... it's okay, come here," Bre said, bending down next to me, her voice quavering.

Her eyes were bloodshot, mascara leaving a trail down to her jawline. She embraced me and rubbed my hair as we silently mourned together, the rhythmic bobbing of our shoulders being the most evident sign of our despair.

Bre had been so strong for me during that time. She'd driven me, taken charge to ensure Mona had the send-off she deserved, and consoled me at least a dozen times. Meanwhile, nobody had been there for her. At least right then, we could finally support each other. I wasn't being strong like I should, but I turned to hug her face to face so that she knew she could be as broken as I was and not be alone for once.

"I miss her so much," Bre whispered, rubbing under her eyes with a tissue.

Sniffling, she then blotted my eyes as I let out a pathetic chuckle.

"You don't have to do that."

"Somebody has to. You look like shit," she said with a little laugh, fresh tears rolling down her cheeks.

I heard Dan clear his throat, and we looked at him standing by the door. People were filing out behind him, breaking left and right into the parking lot.

"We have to go to the graveyard now... just one last goodbye," he said, the final word coming out choked.

The three of us stood together and walked to the parking lot toward Bre's car, needing this time for our own private vigil. As we got in, the sky opened up again, weeping mournful tears in line with my own. I needed to hold on for just a little bit longer.

I slumped down in the front seat and pulled my jacket over my face, withdrawing into isolation. Bre's hand rested on the gear shifter after she'd put the car in drive, and I reached my pinky finger out from under my jacket and interlaced it with hers. We were in this together.

***

"WE'RE HERE. COME ON."

The jacket was pulled away from me, and I winced at the sudden brightness. Outside, it was misty, combined with a dense fog, gravestones jutting out like faceless sentinels awaiting our procession.

My breath caught when I spotted the gnarled tree with thick intertwined branches about head height from the ground. Like a flash, I remembered that I'd been here once before; Mona and I had parked there early in our relationship. Young adults without a place of their own needed to find an escape—that had been ours. It had been our first time under that tree, probably not our best moment and potentially a bad omen, but our first time nonetheless. I could almost feel the warmth of her bare skin against mine... the steaming up of the windows.

Another wave of nausea hit me then. I shouldn't be here, in a place with such ghosts of the past. Mona should be here.

"Trev?" Bre asked, and I flinched, having been too deep in the memory.

"Hmm? Oh yeah, okay, we're here." I made eye contact with Bre. Her face was puffy and ashen but finally dry. There were only so many tears one body could release. I owed her so much for being my rock through this. "Thank you... for everything. Bre, I'm sorry I haven't been stronger. I really can never express to you how much your being here means to me."

"Oh God, no. I lost my sister, but—she was the love of your life. You should be a mess."

I was unable to choke out a reply.

"You know," she continued, "seeing how much you loved her makes me happier than you could ever imagine—" Her voice broke, the strength leaving her as she descended into tearless sobs, her shoulders trembling.

"God, look at me, I'm a mess," she said, sniffling and wiping her nose with a tissue.

"I don't have any tears left either," I said, sighing a breath that took more effort than it should have. I felt like a gorilla was on my chest.

"Shall we?" she asked, opening her car door.

I nodded and began to sweat, hot moisture building under my arms as the panic of facing all of those people again settled in.

"I can't believe how much this is costing," I heard Mona's father say as he walked past Bre's car in the parking lot, as if nothing else was more important.

I'd give any sum of money to have just one more moment with her—hell, I always had. I lived to give her the world.

"Your father's an asshole."

Bre nodded as she shut her car door and sighed. Mona always hated it when I made comments like that, but somebody needed to.

Dan got out of the backseat and opened my door for me. He was grinning, but his face was haggard and pale; he hadn't been sleeping. Another person suffering but carrying on to make sure I did, too.

"Come on, buddy. She's waiting for you."

I couldn't help but share an upturned lip: the mourner's smile.

THOSE WERE the same words Dan had used when I got nervous on our wedding day.

Up to that point, my life with Mona had been a dream. Sure, there were the occasional spats like any couple, but I knew I was the luckiest man alive. Mona filled me with joy, and she loved me truly and unconditionally. It was a feeling I hadn't experienced since my mom died: that sense that no matter what setback might come my way, she would be my cheerleader, propping me up to take that next step forward.

Then there was her father. I'd had so many arguments with that man, and the night before our wedding, at our rehearsal dinner, no less, he'd railed about the irresponsibility of my career choices.

"A writer? It's time to grow up, Trevor," he'd said, never once looking in my direction. "You've had a few little stories, but it's time to get a real job. You're lucky I was around to pay for this wedding."

John waved over one of the servers to bring another tray of hors d'oeuvres as I balled my fists behind my back. That's how it was with him; a complete lack of respect. It was funny that, shortly after the wedding, I'd sell my first book. It was by no means a *New York Times* bestseller, but it did fill the bill to support us. In that moment, though, I'd wanted to defend myself.

"With all due respect, John, I've had more than a few little stories. I—"

"What's going on over here?" Mona asked, looking radiant, gray eyes sparkling. I felt her hand close around my fist and give it a reassuring squeeze.

John finally looked in our direction and his furrowed brow smoothed out, revealing his gentler side. She could always make him melt.

"Darling! We were talking about your husband-to-be's writing."

"What about it?"

Her father's eyes had narrowed at her tone.

"Honey, listen—"

"No, Dad, you listen. I'm not having this, especially the night before our wedding, and that's final."

She pulled me away from the table, my face beaming with triumph.

"I'm so sorry," she started, but I stopped her with a kiss.

"Honey, it's fine. Let's enjoy our night."

I embraced her then, feeling the warmth of her body against mine, that sense of wholeness she always filled me with.

We stood that way for several moments, the opening verses of our favorite song playing faintly in the background.

Fly me away...

Mona had looked at me for a long time then. I wasn't sure what she'd seen on my face that night; fury, I assumed, since I was still pissed at her father. But she had known me better than I'd known myself. There was something there that drew her attention—I could tell by the way her brows scrunched. Had it been doubt she'd observed? Then again, how often was somebody serious when they said "It's fine"?

Whatever it was, she'd been on to something. The following day, amid the flurry of final preparations at the church, it took hold of me: a hesitation. I still didn't know what to call the feeling, but it sent chills down my spine.

"Trev, come on, man," Dan had said, standing on the other side of the church's bathroom door. "Let me in."

"I can't go out there," I said.

A brown-eyed, black-haired man stared back at me in the mirror. It was me, yet not quite. I'd felt like I was out of my body, like some weird kind of déjà vu that was preventing me from moving forward, my skin shuddering with horripilation.

Bang.

"Did you just try to bust the door down?" I asked.

"Yeah. Dammit, I hurt my shoulder."

"Idiot," I said.

"Me? You're the one who's basically saying you won't marry Mona," Dan said.

I swiveled to the door, jerking it open. "I never said that."

Dan adjusted his tux and leveled his eyes on me, raising his left eyebrow.

"Then what do you call this?" he asked, waving his hands around the bathroom. "Locking yourself in here and saying you can't go out there?"

Brushing my fingers through my hair, I'd leaned back against the door.

"I just have this strange feeling. It's like... Ah, I can't put my finger on it. Not dread, but"—I raised my hands to gesticulate my point—"foreboding?"

Dan rolled his eyes.

"Trev, man, it's Mona. Is it her dad? You aren't marrying him."

Initially, I thought he had something to do with it. That ceaseless picking at everything I was doing every time he saw me had been grating my nerves, leaving me resentful—but that was directed at him, not at Mona. No, the feeling that had me in a vice was different.

"It's not that..."

"Oh," Dan said, grabbing my shoulder and giving it a squeeze. "Man, I wasn't thinking. It's about your mom, isn't it?"

"I—" I started to answer, but I couldn't finish. Was that what it was, the fear of more loss? His words struck me like a blow right to the gut. Yes, that had to be it. I'd loved Mona more than life itself; she'd become my only reason for living, and I'd let myself fall into the trap of my own making. After my mother's death, I knew better than to let somebody into my heart, to get too close, yet I swung those metaphorical doors right open for Mona. If I'd lost her, it would, without any doubt, be the end of me. There'd be no coming back from the brink.

"Don't let that hold you back from life. Come on, buddy. She's waiting for you."

· · ·

BRACING MYSELF, I stepped out into the misty cemetery, a low rumble of thunder breaking the silence as the onlookers materialized in the fog.

If I'd listened to my gut feeling all those years ago, would Mona still be here? It was a stupid thought, as if her fate could really be sealed by marrying me, but one I couldn't help dwelling on. I trembled as another peal of thunder permeated the space around us like the crash of a pan in a small room, the fog trapping it in like a box.

I followed the casket as the pallbearers carried it to Mona's final resting place: a person-sized hole surrounded by a varying array of headstones from new to weathered, with an empty green plot next to it that was secured for me. It's ridiculous that cemeteries prey on those in mourning with two-for-one specials. Still, I couldn't stomach anyone else getting that sacred plot beside her for eternity; that space was for me. So I took advantage, though Mona would need to wait a bit longer for me to be at her side.

The pallbearers set Mona's casket down on the wooden struts above her plot and dispersed into the gathering of onlookers. Bre approached then and wrapped her arm around me; her head lowered solemnly as we took our place next to the casket. The priest rested his hand on my shoulder, a gesture meant to comfort me, before he turned away to face the casket and began a final prayer, our last farewell.

All I could think about was the mist accumulating on my face, mixing with my tears, diluting my grief. Its cold essence washed away the final vestiges of my warmth.

The ground shook as another peal of thunder reverberated around us, startling the priest. He adjusted his glasses, wiping away the condensation, and continued, his words lulling me into a trance, like a snake charmer with his flute.

Everything changed then—or, rather, my surroundings looked the same, but something felt different. I wish I could say it was an inner peace, but that wasn't the case. It was more of an ominous sensation tugging at me, beckoning me to my wife's side while the Lord's Prayer rang loudly in my ears.

I tried to fight it; I couldn't face her like this. I dreaded seeing her in her casket with every ounce of my being, but I was in a state of compulsion. There would be no closure unless I laid my eyes upon her one last time.

When the priest finished making the sign of the cross, I held up my hand as if I were a boy back in Sunday school, only this time I was seeking permission for something I was in complete control of. The eyes of dozens of onlookers pivoted to me, my hand a beacon, the lighthouse in the fog signaling all ships in peril to my harbor for safety. Except I wasn't a haven but a harbinger of something more perilous.

"Father, I know this is unorthodox, but... I need to see Mona."

The faces in the crowd ranged from concern to tearful bewilderment. Opening a casket before it's about to be buried is highly unusual.

"Trevor, my son. I don't think—"

I grabbed his cassock, and his eyes widened. It was a move of desperation, not intimidation, but my actions had the latter effect.

The priest cleared his throat and patted my hands, a bead of sweat dripping down his brow.

"As you wish."

I could feel my arms shaking like I'd had too much Redbull; pulses of electricity were coursing through my fingers. I needed to calm down. Mona needed to know I could be her Trevor without her, a man who could live a life as a soloist after the duet's final show.

I began to hum our song, that melody of peace we played when we needed to escape.

Fly me away...

I released the priest's garb, lowering my eyes in repentance as he lifted the cover of the casket.

Mona's parents stepped forward quickly, their umbrellas raised to prevent her body from getting wet, all the while staring at me as though I'd lost touch with my senses.

Her father mumbled; I assumed he was meaning to curse me for my disrespect or something close to it, but Bre grabbed his arm, her eyes menacing.

I nodded to her appreciatively, took a deep breath, and stepped up to the casket's side.

I nearly lost my footing. Mona's body wasn't there.

Where was she? Was this some sick joke?

John scoffed as I looked at him. Did he do this?

I scanned the faces around me, all of them looking into the casket's cavernous depths, their emotions erupting anew, all seeing what I could not.

Rrrriiiippppp.

A tearing sound, like that of fabric, emanated from within. I stepped back, bumping into someone as the sound grew louder and a pointed shadow began ascending from the lining.

Seconds passed, but I didn't notice; it was as though time completely stilled as the object rose higher and higher, nobody in the crowd but me noticing the devilry before them.

A gentle breeze began to flow outward, spiraling the mist and brushing my hair, the smell of gasoline wafting through the air.

The tearing noise ceased.

A white doorway, no different from the size and shape of the one in our bedroom at home, stood open before me. It resided right where Mona's body should have been, the frame of the door embedded in the torn fabric, anchoring it to the coffin's interior. Its hinges creaked as the open door bumped in rhythm with my heart against the lip of the coffin, preventing it from swinging open fully.

I continued to look around, my head whipping from side to side, but nobody else was moving. Their expressions of sorrow were frozen in place, just like the misty raindrops hovering in the air, their glistening reminiscent of stars in a night sky. I waved my hand and the drops in its path moved, leaving a streak of dry space in front of me.

"Jesus Christ in heaven," I whispered.

Life is full of moments that nobody would believe unless they saw it. And despite the slew of people who had the potential to witness this living episode of the *Twilight Zone*, nobody did. They were all statues, from Bre, holding a tissue to her right eye, to John, scowling at me, his eyes unblinking and full of malice.

And what of Monaciel, my love? A doorway was all there was to see where she should be: one that was open, somewhat invitingly, with an eerie, white glow and the smell of car fuel wafting out toward me.

I took a breath and gingerly stepped forward, to the coffin's edge. It felt like a make-or-break moment, something Mona wanted me to see. And so, without giving myself another chance to reconsider, I crossed the event horizon. Placing my foot on the lip of the coffin, I pushed my leg down with all my strength and used that leverage to vault myself through the doorway and into darkness.

FOG SURROUNDED ME.

My ears were muffled, the faint echoes of a song playing in the darkness.

"Hello? Can anyone hear me?"

I tried to move but couldn't feel whether I'd done so. Everything was so light, like I wasn't a part of my own body.

"Mona?"

Something rumbled as the fog began to roil. A cascade of cold slammed into my sense of being, taking my breath away. I couldn't inhale, my lungs burning as the world grew dim. I opened my mouth to scream, and mist invaded me, rushing down my esophagus, its iciness cutting my throat as it went down.

This couldn't be happening. Was I dying? I'd never dreamed this would be my end.

Fly me away. From this cold, dark place...

The song punctuated my pain but also ended it. I could feel my body again, could feel my eyes blinking as a blurry image came into view.

The song continued.

A bright escape. It's time to change my fate, today...

No, no, no, no...

Gigi McLean, her voice haunting and isolating in those opening words. On so many nights, this song played while we drank wine and ate cheese on our patio, enjoying the warmth, just being together.

I couldn't bear this. I willed for this place to release me, but the world coalesced instead.

I was in a car, my hands on the steering wheel, the dash illuminated by the speedometer and the central infotainment screen. The air was cool on my skin from the lowered window on my left, a weird yet comforting juxtaposition with the heat blowing on my feet. Mona's feet had always been cold.

It was dark, with headlights from the cars in the other lane passing by intermittently being the only reprieve. I took a curve smoothly, nothing but an ocean of darkness on my right aside from a lone sign close to the road's edge.

California State Route I.

"No... God, no. Please," I said, beginning to understand what I was bearing witness to.

My hands were firmly in place on the steering wheel: ten and two. Mona never sacrificed safety, always willing to throw out self-deprecating comments about her old-lady driving habits. She had been so careful, going five miles per hour over the speed limit only when she felt extraordinarily rushed.

"Mona, stop the car! Please," I yelled—or at least I tried to, the force of my action feeling like it should have come out as loudly as the foghorn on a barge, but no sound accompanied it. The only sensations were the wind, the road, and Gigi McLean.

My hand—no, *her* hand—reached over to turn the volume knob on the console, her slender fingers rotating the dial as the tempo of the song increased to something peppier. The solitaire on her ring finger glistened as she tapped on the steering wheel to the beat.

It was then that I could see them in her periphery: the swerving lights. This was how it happened; all the pieces were there. Mona's executioner was coming, and I couldn't stop him.

I never could imagine what it must be like to be paralyzed, to have the mental capacity to think about moving a part of my body but to not be able to do so. And, to my horror, I was no longer ignorant of that scenario; I couldn't move. I might as well have been a silent bystander to a crime, one of those people you see on TV recording an incident on their phone rather than doing a damn thing to stop it.

Everything was unraveling.

Our focus shifted to look up at the exit sign, Mona not noticing the oncoming driver's erratic swerving. Ten miles. Oh, God, this is where it happened.

Time sped up now, details becoming blurred as the events unfolded. The sign became brighter as if lit by a spotlight activated just for her. An inhalation. Startlement. I could sense her fright.

Our center of focus shifted, not so much with her eyes but her whole body, as an exerted force rotated us from the sign to the twin bright lights, to darkness, and then to the stars, an array of the galaxy's beauty swirling around us as weightlessness took over. Strands of her dark blonde hair floated around her face as her gaze met her own reflection in the rearview mirror.

We stared at each other, or at least I stared through her eyes, for only a fraction of a second, but in that time, her expression went from terror to recognition with a subtle furrowing of her forehead, just like the night of our rehearsal dinner. She saw me. She knew I was there with her. Didn't she?

"*I'm right here, baby. I'm coming with you.*" Again, my voice was absent.

Her eyebrows shot up in surprise as her lips parted—

Everything went black.

A cacophony of tearing metal and physics in action erupted as the car rolled—three times, investigators would later say, but the rotations were indecipherable to me in that moment—before plunging off SR 1 to the rocky shore thirty feet below.

Red, a color I would never be able to view the same way again, tinted everything. I tried to squint and blink it away, but it came and went at various degrees of intensity, the air thick with the smell of burning oil and gasoline.

Gasps and suction. A struggle for breath. She was with me in her body, but I couldn't look at her face, see into her eyes; I couldn't tell her that I wouldn't leave her to die alone. All of that was withheld from me as I remained a passenger within her skin.

I could feel her body start to fail, coming in fits and starts like a lawn mower as its fuel ran dry, sputtering with a few good attempts before faltering with a final drawn-out gasp.

Red slowly started to fade to black, as a break in the color revealed her reflection in the dangling review mirror. Her bloody eye drooped closed as the radio, still functioning, played the final verse of our song, slow and haunting once more.

Fly me away. From this cold, dark place. A bright escape. It's time to change my fate, today...

SEARING pain tore through my abdomen as I was yanked backward through the doorway. I swung my arms, trying to fight off my assailant, that unseen entity who took me away from Mona, but my flailing appendages sailed uninterrupted through the cool air.

The pulling stopped, and I dropped to my knees on the damp grass of the graveyard, too weak to stand without support.

Cccreeeaaakkk.

An icy gust blew through my hair toward the door, as if the phantom who extricated me was fleeing back to its domain, the door slamming shut by the power of its movement.

Boom.

Shouts of startlement rang out around me as all the mourners started to move, the ground shuddering in concert with the crack of thunder. Time had restarted, and the door was gone. The priest was lowering the lid to the casket with a slow shake of his head. Such a shame, he must have thought.

"No," I said, my voice a hoarse whisper.

I tried to stand but my legs didn't want to cooperate, wobbling like jelly before giving out again.

"Mona—," I choked out.

"I know, Trev."

Hands clasped under my arms, gently aiding me to my feet.

Tears clouded my sight, but I knew that voice.

"Dan, did you see it?"

He was silent. I turned to him and he watched me, eyes narrowed.

"What?" I asked when he didn't say anything.

"We've all seen her, Trevor. That was hard for us all to see again."

I looked around. Fresh tears were on every face, even John's. Bre was watching Dan and me, her eyes bloodshot and puffy.

"Not her. The other—In the casket. Didn't you—?"

Dan's furrowed brows deepened as he released his hold on me. I grabbed his hand with both of mine, shaking it, willing him to hear me.

"The door, Dan. The fucking door!"

He tried to unlatch my grip, wide-eyed, head swiveling slowly in disbelief.

"Trev, it's only a casket holding your wife. Nothing more."

"No!"

Dan took a step back, his hands finally freed of mine. "I know this is hard—"

"No...," I said, turning to face it. "Open it again. I'm not crazy. I'll show you."

He patted my shoulder but kept his body distant.

"At this point, that's not a good idea. I think... I think you need some rest. Mona needs to rest, Trevor."

"But I swear... I—I'm not making this up. I saw it. I saw everything that happened to her..."

"I saw her too afterward, remember? My imagination ran wild with what that must have been like. But, Trev, there is nothing in there other than her."

My shoulders hunched, the gravity of what I'd seen weighing on me. Was it all in my head?

Dan moved in closer, his voice lowering to just above a whisper. "Everyone's been through enough."

He smiled at me, a pantomime of reassurance and friendliness, while his voice was tinged with something colder.

I looked away, unable to bear his ruse, and took in the crowd; concerned expressions and silence greeted me. Everyone stood stock-still except the brave few who gingerly approached me as if I were a cornered dog.

What had I looked like to them?

"Just get me out of here," I said, seeing that nothing I said would change the fact that I alone witnessed what happened to her; only I saw Mona die.

"Come on," Dan said, giving me a nudge. I acquiesced, allowing him to guide me away.

Thunder boomed off in the distance, and I turned my head to peer at the casket one last time. Could it—? No, the lid was still closed. Maybe I *was* just the mourner dancing on the edge of sanity.

Sighing, I put one foot in front of the other, marching away from Mona's side, the acrid smell of burning oil and flesh lingering in the afternoon breeze.

LIFE ENDED that day for me, or at least it seemed to. Days passed without me uttering a word or eating, with the curtains drawn to blot out the world. Nothing could replace the light Mona had brought to my life.

Time was indistinct, a concept that lost all meaning as I still felt trapped in her head, watching her demise. Who could continue after that?

The phone rang often. I never answered it or bothered to see who it was. I'm sure Dan and Bre were amongst my callers, trying to figure out if I was getting out of bed. Most days I did, but I never ventured much further than the couch. The air in my living room was cool and musty. It was like a tomb.

One morning, a banging woke me as I lay in my cocoon of blankets on the couch.

"Mona?" I called out, looking at my bedroom door from across the room, whose style and shape were eerily reminiscent of the doorway that protruded from her coffin. I pushed the thought away.

I'd returned less and less to our room as each day passed, unable to look at Mona's clothes once I realized they wouldn't conjure her. They were just empty pieces of fabric, never to be filled by her beating heart again.

Bang, bang, bang.

That definitely hadn't come from my bedroom.

"Trevor! Come on, man, open up!"

Dan. I knew he wouldn't stay away.

Bang, bang, bang.

"Are you dead?"

I sighed. Wouldn't he feel like crap if I was?

"Coming," I said, and felt the burn in my throat from lack of use. I didn't even sound like myself, voice hoarse and gravelly.

"Holy sh—," Dan stopped, shaking his head when he saw me. "I thought it would be bad, but Trev, look at you. Have you seen yourself?"

I could have answered him, but his bafflement was enough. I was sure I didn't want to look in a mirror, so I just stared at him, speechless.

He squinted at me and slowly waved his hand back and forth in front of my eyes as if I wasn't there, and he was kind of right in that assumption. I didn't know where I was anymore, feeling more like a specter haunting my home than a living person. Needless to say, it seemed as though I also looked the part.

After a few waves of his hand, I finally shook my head, recoiling back into the living room to escape the brightness of the late-afternoon sun that shined through the front door. "Leave me be."

"Oh no, you don't. We've all left you be for long enough. It's a dick move not to answer your phone and let someone know you're still breathing, you know."

Dan followed me into the living room and switched on the lights.

"My God," he said, mouth agape.

Running his hand through his hair, he powered on.

"Enough is enough." His words were slow and deliberate. "This is not what Mona would want, Trev. You have got to come back to the world of the living. Do you know how many times I've called you—we've called you? I can't even count now. Have you even checked your phone?"

I shook my head, and some tension melted from Dan's face. So he'd been angry with me.

"Well, I'm glad you weren't being a complete asshole."

"Hey—"

"No, Trev. It's been three weeks—three whole weeks of this. You have to realize this is not okay."

Three weeks? I'd known I'd disengaged for a while, even that it might have been a week or two, but three? My agent and editor must be furious.

Dan was nodding at me.

"I'll try," I said, still taken aback.

Reality was a double-edged sword. On the one hand, I didn't want my life to escape me, and it was starting to, but on the other hand, what was life without Mona? Was it even worth my time?

"I smell."

Dan smirked and quite evidently kept his distance.

"Yeah, you do. Go shower. I'll order pizza."

I looked up, somewhat encouraged.

"With pepperoni and—"

"And pineapple. Just the way she liked it. Let's celebrate your coming back to life with her."

I smiled, nodding, starting to feel better.

WATER NEVER FELT BETTER on my skin than in that moment, the warmth rejuvenating my bones. Dan hadn't been kidding; I looked horrible. A scraggly beard and sunken, pale cheeks were my new facade.

I was a walking corpse. Mona wouldn't have recognized me in the slightest. She had always told me her greatest attraction and jealousy was my olive skin tone, courtesy of my Italian roots. That hue was no longer visible; all that remained was an emaciated husk of my former self.

My clothes hung looser on me as I draped them over my frame before exiting the bathroom.

Dan was in the kitchen. He'd cleaned the dishes and set out three plates and wine glasses while decanting a bottle of Merlot.

"Mona's favorite...," I whispered, picking up the empty bottle of Duckhorn from the counter. Dan spun around and smiled.

"I thought it'd be fitting," he said, following my eyes as I looked off past the bottle of wine.

He whistled to get my attention. "We need to remember her while still living, Trev."

I frowned and nodded, feeling the tears welling within and rising to the surface, a geyser preparing to erupt.

The doorbell rang, and Dan seemed unsurprised.

"I got it, buddy. Maybe put some music on."

I winced as Dan squeezed my shoulder on his way to answer the door. I knew he was trying to be reassuring, but not everyone wants to be touched at any given time, and for me, that happened to be one of those moments.

Just shake it off, I told myself, rubbing the place where his hand had been and squeezing my eyes shut.

A flash of stars. Dark blonde hair was suspended around my face. The pain in my shoulder, tight and constricting, and my body straining against the seatbelt, preventing me from being thrown...

I gasped and opened my eyes, unclasping my fingers from my shoulder, which had turned white from the pressure I was applying.

It was Mona again. The memory was just as stark as the day of the funeral when I'd been there with her, forced to watch her death, unable to do anything. She was gone so fast. If only—

"Hey," Dan said as he opened the door, and I hurried over to the record player to put on an album; I didn't need him finding me staring off into space in the middle of my living room, especially when he thought I'd started to do better.

The murmuring continued, so I busied myself, opening the lid to our record crate. The scent of aged paper wafted out at me, not dissimilar to books, and I paused to take it in. There was something else there, too—a stirring, teasing my arm hair to stand on end. It was so subtle I'd almost missed it. Mona. She must be here with me.

My fingers moved of their own accord, brushing against the sleek album covers. Their touch was as familiar to me as the keys of a piano are to a pianist. I stopped when I encountered a roughened edge and pulled that album out.

Miles Davis, *Kind of Blue*. Man, was that an album. A tingle, almost like static, coursed through me as I set the record on the turntable and moved the tonearm into place.

And then a rush hit me—like that stuffed feeling your head gets when you have a cold, but mixed with the mellow, buzzed sensation that comes after an Old Fashioned or two. It was a thrumming in my head, its rhythm alternating to match that of the song and my heart while the world around me was tuned out. That beat, it was almost like...

We lay in our bed while my head rested on Mona's chest; the lub-dub of her heart echoed in my ears, matching the steady beat of the double bass from Miles Davis's song "So What" playing on our record player. Jazz was a hallmark of our relationship, even when we made love. The music made me feel smooth and suave, qualities that wouldn't typically be attributed to me, and while I didn't need it with Mona, the effort made her wild.

She took another deep breath, her chest heaving, in and out, as she tried to catch her breath. I lifted my head to look into her eyes, and I saw only happiness, those pools of her soul that made me feel like the most important man in the world.

"I love you," she said. We kissed and I placed my hand on her breast.

Lub-dub. Lub-dub. Lub-dub.

I felt a presence behind me that pulled me out of my memory, that absence of sound that occurs when a mass moves in from behind and distorts the senses.

Mona?

I swiveled on my feet to face her, and then she was there, standing in front of me. Not an apparition but a real person, the light of the setting sun shining through the open door accentuating her features.

The rhythms grew louder in my ears. It *was* her.

"Trevor," she said, turning completely toward me. The light temporarily blinded me, and then I plummeted.

It had been a trick of the eye: the overlapping image of Mona pulled away and faded into the distinct features of Bre, with her softer cheeks and smoother angles.

Miles sang louder, the sounds around me crisp and distinct. This was all wrong. I shouldn't be listening to these albums without Mona. I couldn't stomach it.

"You could raise the dead with it this loud," Bre said, giving me a smirk and a wink as she turned the dial down. The music receded to a soft, lobby-level ambience.

I could think again, though I didn't want to. It hadn't been the first time I'd mistaken Bre for Mona, though now, with the music's hold on me stripped away, the resemblances between them were even fewer. Bre had a lesser quality, probably much like myself, with her face too wan and paired with discolorations covered by too much makeup. Not quite Meryl and Goldie at the end of *Death Becomes Her*, but I still couldn't help drawing the parallels between the sisters.

"You could raise the dead with it this loud."

Her statement, though used in jest, tugged at me. From the look of us, we all seemed to be on our last legs, but I felt a surge of life when I was vibing with the music, its vibrations tuning me into something greater—to Mona.

Realization dawned on me.

"Well, there he is," Bre said, her face brightening with a large smile to match my own. She pulled me in for an encompassing hug.

I felt smothered and trapped, but I couldn't bring myself to pull away. Bre likely needed the contact as much as I did deep down.

"Well, thanks for making me feel so welcome. All I get is a glower, but you show up, Bre, and he lights up like a Christmas tree," Dan said, shaking his head and carrying the pizzas into the kitchen.

She pulled back, eyes glassy. "Well, I'm glad. I haven't seen enough smiling lately."

"I didn't think those muscles even worked anymore," I said, consciously holding it in place.

My patience was already wearing thin, even though she'd just arrived. In times of crisis, Bre and Dan could be relied upon to be there and show me the path forward. I'd reached a junction, though, and from here on I had to continue alone on my own path.

I ran my fingers through my hair and cleared my throat.

"Let's have some wine."

Bre wiped her eyes.

"That's the best suggestion I've heard all day."

We ate, drank, and laughed, but despite the company, my mind kept wandering away from the present to the open record crate in the living room.

Miles had been switched to Louis Armstrong, followed by John Coltrane and Dizzy Gillespie. All the while, the volume was too low for me to zero in on it, too distant for me to feel its rush.

"Where'd you go?" Dan asked, and my eyes refocused. Both of their looks were trained on me, their expressions relaxed; the aftereffects of several glasses of wine.

I don't know if it was my own lowered inhibitions or my belief that theirs were sufficiently so, but I saw my opportunity to strike, since I knew they wouldn't let me get rid of them yet.

I stood from my chair in the kitchen and walked to the living room, beckoning for them to follow me with the wave of my hand.

"Come on," I said, turning up the music.

"How are we supposed to hear one another?" Bre asked, and Dan snorted, plopping down on the couch that had served as my bed for the better part of the last three weeks.

"I don't think being heard was ever a problem for you."

"Screw off, Dan," Bre said, eyes narrowed.

I raised my hands, palms facing out like a crossing guard.

"Let the music take you and see what happens. Mona and I would do this... just sit and vibe," I said.

Bre raised her glass.

"To Mona."

I nodded and closed my eyes, waiting to be transported away.

The music flowed through me then, like water through a pipe, more utility than beauty. While the sound of the brass with up-tempo percussion made my heart sing, the static, that energy, was nowhere to be seen.

I doubled down, straining to tune out the sounds of Dan's mouth breathing or the rustle of Bre's legs as she rubbed them together.

Focus.

A spark, like the bright initial flash when a wick ignites on a fire-cracker, burst into my mind with the sound of Ella Fitzgerald's strong and pure voice. It pulsed in my mind's eye, hovering in a fog-filled darkness.

Mona, I tried to call out mentally, but static scrambled my voice, the world blurring.

My temples began to throb as I clenched my eyes more tightly shut. I needed to reconnect; I was so close, but the static grew louder, a consistent white noise full of crackles and pops.

"Dammit."

I opened my eyes.

Bre and Dan were watching me, devoid of expression.

"What?" I asked, frowning.

Dan cleared his throat and leaned forward on his knees.

"Well, Trev, you looked in pain, but I guess you seem fine now."

"Yeah, I'm fine," I said, crossing my arms.

Bre's eyebrows raised, and she looked to Dan as he sat back again, lifting his hands as if surrendering.

"Alright, man. You were moving your lips and scrunching your face. We didn't know what was happening."

So much for me moving on from Dan thinking I'd lost it.

I walked to the record player and pulled up the tonearm, plunging the room into uncomfortable silence.

There had to be a way to reach Mona again. It had worked earlier with the Miles record; I had felt her. I know Bre walked in, but Mona had been with me; I could swear it. I heard her beat.

Taking a deep breath, I faced them. Dan's eyes were crinkled with concern, but Bre's held curiosity.

Lub-dub. It was so quiet I almost missed it, but that beat was there again when I met Bre's gaze. Mona was telling me to trust her sister; what else could it mean? Why else could I hear the beat again, no matter how faint, when gazing upon Bre?

"I think I can see Mona," I blurted out.

Dan threw up his hands and stood. "Not this again."

"Hey!" Bre said, cutting him off. "We aren't shaming him for missing his wife."

I motioned for them to stop speaking.

"Bre, thanks, but it's not me just missing her. I saw her at the funeral, and I don't mean in her casket. I saw how she died—like I actually experienced it and was a part of her. I know this sounds bizarre, but I felt that same—" I paused, snapping my fingers, trying to encourage my thoughts to catch up with my mouth, "presence or transcendence,... well, not the same exact thing, but something similar when I played Miles Davis earlier. You know, when you said I could wake the dead."

"Hold up," Bre said, standing to join the rest of us on our feet. "Are you trying to say you manifested my sister somehow?"

"I don't know. I... Something happened; I can't explain it, but it's like she was here with me. It comes and goes. I think it's something with the jazz—"

Dan slammed his drink down, and Bre and I both flinched. We watched him, his face red and angry.

"There was no music at the graveyard. None of this makes sense, Trevor, none of it!"

"Why are you getting so angry?" Bre asked, a question I, too, wanted answered.

"How are you not? This is insane. We've all been here, going above and beyond to help him, meanwhile all having lost a person that was close to us as well, and what? You want me to feed this delusion?"

Dan shifted his attention to me, his hands clenched into fists.

"Well, it's not happening. I'm not here for that."

Silence followed as Bre stepped closer to me, still facing Dan. I took in his posture and attempted dominance, and something snapped inside me. I didn't need someone around who would try to keep me from my wife.

I sat back down in my chair.

"Get out," I said, flicking my hand toward the door.

Dan stared at me for several seconds, eyes locked with mine, before he looked to Bre, bewildered.

"Don't look to her for help," I said, my voice steady and quiet, just barely audible. "Get out and don't come back."

Bre looked at me, her inner turmoil evident.

"Trevor, I know he's being—"

"Bre," I cut her off. "I just want to be alone right now. Could you also go? I'll call you."

Affronted, she put her hand to her chest, opening her mouth to protest, but she must have thought better of it. Looking to the ground in defeat, she nodded.

Dan followed her out, his eyes wide with shock. Nobody spoke.

I kept my gaze fixed on the door, ensuring nobody would storm into my house in a flurry of protests, and stayed that way for several minutes. I didn't have the patience for interruptions.

Once satisfied that they were truly gone and not coming back, I hurried to the record player as though making up for lost time, desperate to draw her out.

Mona, my love, I'm going to find you.

I MOVED like a man possessed as I switched from one record to the next, trying desperately to find that spark I'd felt earlier. Classic or contemporary, it didn't matter. But nothing happened and hysteria set in, spurring me forward in an incomprehensible flurry of meaningless action.

Streetlights extinguished, their light retreating from that of the rising sun while the pile of played records grew until only one remained.

Gigi McLean.

It always came back to Gigi. If there was one album, and even more than that, one song, that we played together more than any other, it was the one on this record.

Fly me away...

A part of me had known it would be the key to play it as soon as I'd felt my connection with Miles, realizing the music tied to our memories together completed the circuit like the filament in a light bulb, that tiny thread needed to make light, but my hand strayed away every time as if of its own accord, goose bumps dotting my arm when it would draw too close, an unseen barrier warning me of danger. But with no other option remaining, I needed to try.

My fingers closed around the record sleeve, and as I applied pressure to pinch it and lift it out of the crate, my grip slipped as though it was lined in jelly.

Rubbing my hands on my shirt, I tried again, and the resistance increased, shifting from an inability to touch the record to a pit in my stomach that had me doubled over, unable to reach my arm forward. I curled in on myself.

"Mona," I said, her name leaving my lips as no more than an utterance that echoed like a cymbal in my quiet home.

My frequency took on visual form as her name vibrated in the air, a ripple that expanded into translucent waves that blanketed the room. The pain in my gut lessened.

I uttered her name over and over, louder with each breath, manifesting her into being with the force of my words.

"Mona, Mona, Mona—"

The sound waves became more solid, slick to the touch like sheets of ice I could run my hands along, angling inward toward the record case and Gigi McLean.

My hand closed around it, placed it on the player, lowered the tonearm, and—

FOG SURROUNDED ME.

The sound was muted, the faint echoes of a song playing in the darkness, its words nearly indiscernible. No, not just any song.

Fly me away. From this cold, dark place...

I held my tongue, remembering the knives of pain rushing down my throat the last time. I didn't know how I would talk to her, to save her, but I'd been given another chance. I couldn't squander it.

A bright escape. It's time to change my fate, today...

The fog shifted, disturbed by a blast of wind that had no end, parting around me. I felt like Moses in the Red Sea as a black chasm opened between two walls of swirling darkness.

I reached out and could feel the cool mist brushing against me, the wetness seeping into my being.

It was different this time, I realized, as the wind buffeted me and the clouds parted, revealing a rocky shore. I was like a vulture soaring high above, waiting for death to take those on the ground.

Where was Mona? Why wasn't I with her?

A car materialized far below me, cruising along a dark, unlit road, winding through one turn after another. I shivered violently and felt goose bumps race up my arms.

It was her, it was Mona. I couldn't do anything to help up here in the sky. Why is it happening like this?

I willed myself forward, but I moved no closer; the car distorted like the image on an old television that needed the antennas adjusted.

Fly me away...

Gigi's voice had changed, morphing into something deep and menacing. The phrase repeated over and over again in slow motion before merging into a constant rumble, drowning out my thoughts. Then, a new sound.

Trevor!

Mona? Had she called for me?

I tried to concentrate, to steady the image of the car in my mind, but its rippling image was distorted further. The world became static, and suddenly, I plunged into darkness with the scratch of a record resonating in my ears and the faint smell of burning oil tickling my nose.

MY TEMPLES PULSED, a migraine blooming in my head. Light shone through the front windows, the rays stabbing at me like nails to my corneas, halting my ability to think.

I closed my eyes and crawled to the windows, flailing my arms about to grab the curtains and slide them closed. I nearly tore down the rod they were affixed to.

I lay down and took steady breaths: a long inhale, then an exhale. I did this for several minutes while rubbing my forehead, trying to make sense of what had happened. The last I remembered, I was back in that other place where Mona died, but it was so different. Instead of being with Mona, I was high above, unable to reach her, and then the static, like the video feed had been cut. None of it made sense.

I should have been with her, been a part of her like before. What happened? Why did it change from her funeral? I couldn't change Mona's fate from the clouds; I needed to be with her again, in the car. If I could just get closer to her somehow like I was the first time when I was pulled through the doorway. I knew there had to be a way.

Despite the feeling that the answer was shadowed and unseen, almost within my grasp, I at least knew I'd found the key to that place: the way to saving Mona, even if, for now, she was just out of reach. I would try again and again if I had to. I would get there eventually, to her. Gigi McLean was my key.

I sat upright slowly as the pressure in my head increased with every inch I moved until I was completely vertical, taking in the room with squinted eyes.

Records were scattered about the room, not a single one remaining in the crate, and the record player was upside down on the floor, its tonearm snapped off and discarded to the side like a piece of refuse. I didn't recall doing that, but at least—oh no, the record.

Flipping the turntable over, I found the Gigi McLean album smashed, its single piece becoming four. Without it, I had no way to reach Mona.

I crawled around the room, pushing through the pain splitting through my skull as I searched for my phone. I needed to order another copy immediately. That was my only hope.

Knocking over a TV tray, I found my phone lying face down. I had several new texts, almost all of them from Bre. Time was too precious to waste for the single text from Dan, but Bre, I owed her the courtesy of reading what she had to say for taking my side the night before.

BRE
11:47 PM

Hey. I know you've been going through a lot, so know that I'm here for you.

This whole situation sucks. Dan's being spastic and

well this doesn't make sense, but I would never doubt you. Mona always believed in you

11:58 PM

Just let me know if you want to talk. I'll listen, Trev

1:42 AM

Have you heard of noise therapy or sound healing? It's pretty interesting—something to look into?

So certain frequencies can relieve stress. Others can heal your body, and still, even higher frequencies can eliminate guilt. What if that's the key to seeing Mona?

2:41 AM

Someone on Reddit claims to have seen a
loved one when doing Shamanic sound
healing. Have you done this? I can't wrap my
head around how you saw her at the
graveyard, but maybe there was something
else?

3:01 AM

Jesus, I've gone down a rabbit hole. Just call
me, okay? I miss her so much...

Bre believed me. I knew what I was claiming was outlandish, but I know what I saw. It had to be real. Even so, deep down, I didn't blame Dan for reacting like he did. I likely would have done the same. But finally, I had someone on my side. A link to Mona, her sister, encouraging me to continue my search. To find her.

"Shamanic sound healing," I said aloud into Siri, my headache subsiding with my new sense of purpose, soothing my pain like a salve to a wound.

I dove into the search results, scanning page after page with unrestrained enthusiasm. The communion with nature and evocation of the spirit world tugged at my curiosity; had I somehow done this without knowing?

The unfortunate hallmarks of my life had been trauma, that lesion that can destroy the soul and the psyche, and in these trials, I had lost my way. All those nights mourning my mother and feeling alone, a child on a rudderless boat in the dark. It was jazz, that emotional sound that drilled down to the depths of my being, that I tethered to pull myself back from the abyss.

Had I made an otherworldly connection?

That time in my life, after my mother had passed, was so hazy that I couldn't even summon an image—just the sweet song of the brass calling me home: sax, trumpet, and a throaty trombone. But then Mona's death happened. What did that do to my connection with jazz? Did the return of my sorrow with Mona's loss taint the music that was once my salvation so that I could only bear witness to her death, or did it open a gateway for me to save her?

Fear and doubt wormed their way into my thoughts until a melancholic fog was all that remained.

I closed my web browser. Shamanic sound healing wasn't the answer. I had been trying to make an idea a reality, but that didn't make it true. Bre was on to something, though. I could feel it, an itch between my shoulder blades.

I stood and nudged my foot against the record player. It was busted, a rattle, like shaking a container of breath mints, emanating from my little tap.

"We always have the music in us," Mona's favorite adage every time we were away and I felt a little blue, came back to me. The rhythm, that beat, pumped life into me just as she had, her essence acting as my proverbial defibrillator. Her energy was intoxicating.

I'd been a better man with her, someone worth being around, but I had my moments even then.

She loved being out in the wilderness, our backyard a haven for such beauty with us being in central California. When we'd find those places of solitude, my world felt fuller than being in the heart of any city.

I admit the initial seclusion terrified me, afraid of what my own thoughts would bring, but when I was with Mona, that fear was brushed aside every time. That was her. Her light, her goodness, could fill any vacuum and make any place feel like enough.

Mona sought out those places devoid of civilization's hustle and bustle to embrace nature's music, just she and I. And, without prompt, she'd grab my hand, move it in a gentle rat-a-tat-tat motion, and say, "We always have the music in us."

I believed her, internalizing her sermon to the point of it being true. But without her, my band director, I was faced with bone-chilling silence.

I CARRIED on as day turned to night and then back again, all the while lyrics to songs and wisps of melody floated through my mind. I tried to grasp each one, to embrace the tune, but each was carried away on the breeze in my audible defeat. I couldn't recall them, not enough without the record player amplifying the tracks to feel that pulse of bass in my veins.

I sighed, and soon, those turned to yawns. Another half a day passed, and that electricity, that presence—Mona's essence—hadn't returned.

"I need a drink," I muttered.

My phone rang as I dropped ice cubes in my glass.

"Perfect timing...," I said sarcastically. Why couldn't I just be left alone?

"What? Hello, Trevor?"

I put the bottle of vodka down without pouring it and cleared my throat.

"Hi, Bre. Sorry, nothing. What's up?"

I felt the heat in my cheeks as though I'd already had a cocktail and took a seat at the table.

"Hey, so I don't mean to bother you—well, I guess I do, since I called," she laughed. Her tone sounded forced. "Anyway, did you read my texts about the sound healing?"

"I did," I said, feeling apprehension churning in my gut.

"Okay... Well, what do you think?"

"I... I don't know."

"You said the music brought her to you—"

"I did, yes, but what about the graveyard? Dan was right. There wasn't music there," I said, my voice rising. I felt a tug at the back of my mind as those words left my mouth, though I didn't know why. Was there music?

I pinched my arm, digging my nails in until I wanted to cry out. Bre wasn't the enemy here; she couldn't help my failure. Why couldn't I get Mona to come back?

She let out a long breath.

"I get that. I'm just... I'm trying to help."

"I know," I said, wiping tears with my free hand. "Why do you believe me, Bre?"

"Because—" I could hear her swallow, voice taking on the weight of her sorrow. "I can't let her go either."

We were quiet for a while, holding the line, but neither of us said anything; we just breathed and grieved.

"I'm sorry about—" I finally said, breaking the silence.

"Don't. It's okay. I get it."

"Sound healing, huh?"

Bre laughed. It was tinged with grief, but I could feel the warmth too—the hope.

"I didn't hear any ideas from you. It was really interesting, though, about the different sound waves. They believe the hertz levels can trigger a different form of healing."

"It sounds a bit New Agey to me—"

"And saying you are seeing a firsthand account of your wife's death doesn't seem outlandish?" she asked.

Before I could interject, she continued.

"Anyway, I couldn't really determine what Shamanic sound healing entailed, but online, there were a bunch of options to book Zoom sessions to do it. Honestly, I don't really understand how it works."

I nodded as she spoke. "Me either. What are these frequencies you mentioned?"

"I'm glad you asked," she said, her cadence picking up speed. "I know you said it came and went when you mentioned sensing her last night, but maybe it's the record player. It doesn't play the music clearly enough, you know, with the frequencies. And guess what, it's the modern age, Trev. You have streaming apps, which coincidentally stream at a significantly improved frequency."

"Okay, and?"

"Play the songs on your phone," she said exasperatedly. "Supposedly, there are playlists at 963 hertz, which they call the God frequency, that is supposed to open you to spiritual connections."

I frowned and could feel my shoulders tensing, my body's

response to something I was rejecting. I didn't have room to dismiss an idea out of turn.

"These sounds aren't jazz, though. Besides, there's a song we would listen to together, and that specifically... I think that might be the bridge to Mona. My record got smashed after you and Dan left, but right before it did, I'd played it, and I could feel, I don't know exactly how to describe it... a current? It was like the air was electrified."

"Did you see her?"

"No, at least not like the first time. I was so high above her I could only faintly see her car below me, and then everything went fuzzy, kind of like when I was a kid and we had to adjust the antennas on the TV. The world went staticky, and I lost the picture."

"Whoa," she said, and I could hear the sound of her fingers on a keyboard. "What if you played that song and the playlist at the same time or had them blend from one into the other? Like the 963 hertz playlist to open your mind and then the song to, I don't know, transport you or whatever."

Like that first star in the night sky, a glimmer peeked through the darkness, illuminating my despair with the faintest sense of possibility.

Mona, there may be hope.

"Well, I'll let you go," Bre said. I could tell she was eager for me to try our plan. And I had to admit, I was thankful. Usually, I would have rolled my eyes and made some joke about getting out the incense and crystals, but my life had taken a turn I never would have expected.

I CLOSED MY EYES, posture straight against the seat back as the meditative sound of the Solfeggio frequencies resonated through me.

It was time to lower my barriers of apprehension and doubt. The skeptic needed to become the conduit. I let go.

I had some difficulty at first; the alien sounds were more akin to what I imagined a whale to sound like beneath the waves than the frequency of a higher plane of being, but soon, I was lulled into it. I felt light enough to float out of my seat and be carried away by a breeze. Light as a feather, stiff as a board.

I chuckled, or I tried to, but my throat tickled enough that I couldn't produce sound. The pulses shimmying across my appendages led to an itch I couldn't scratch.

Vibrations rippled through the air.

The windowpanes hummed in their casements, much like a gong when lightly brushed. The faint rumbling of the music rolled off in tiny sonic booms that blanketed my body more fiercely. The sound flowed from one end of the room to the other, bouncing from object to object and then back again like a life-sized Newton's cradle.

My head became fuzzy and the world grew opaque in my mind's eye. A door formed in front of me—that same white door I'd seen in the graveyard—but I couldn't find the way in. A vertical rippling wall blocked my path, its surface identical to a pond in a rainstorm, expanding circles of movement branching out in all directions.

I reached out, certain it was an illusion, a deterrent to keep the weak away, but its heat scalded me, a blast of hot steam burning my hand from several feet away as its surface roiled.

Cradling my hand, I stepped backward, and my back met a vibrating barrier, trapping me in.

I knew there had to be a way out. That frequency wouldn't last forever. I slumped, the heat taking on weight as the air grew thick with condensation, each revolution of sound exponentially increasing its pull.

I fell to my knees, unable to lift my head, when suddenly, the sound stopped.

It was abrupt, but its effects were immediate, with the crushing pressure falling away like unlocked shackles.

I sucked in a loud and cool breath.

The walls were still, the final ripples ironing out into smooth panes of smoked glass on either side of me. The door was there, just out of reach.

Fly me away...

Gigi McLean, right on cue.

The lyric resonated faintly in the still air, the condensation solidifying into wisps of fog. The temperature plummeted, and whiffs of gasoline started to reach my nose.

I wasn't sure exactly how this would play out, let alone if I would make it to whatever plane of existence Mona was on, but I knew that Gigi's words would begin sixty seconds after the 963 hertz playlist started. She emerged just in time.

From this cold, dark place...

The fog moved, her voice somehow reversing the ripple effect of the previous playlist so that instead of moving outward, everything began traveling at an inward pulse. It was like hitting rewind on everything I'd just seen.

A bright escape...

The roiling wall in front of me started to freeze as my breath became visible. The ripples moved more slowly as their viscosity increased, and crunchy crystalline noises punctuated the song's eerie call.

My teeth chattered as the sweat on my back and neck froze. I needed to reach that door.

Taking a few steps forward, I could feel the cold wafting at me from the circular-patterned wall in front of me, each step like trudging through a foot of snow, but I continued. I feared that I wouldn't be making it anywhere if I didn't make it through.

It's time to change my fate, today...

I lunged, bracing my shoulder, and shattered the wall of ice like a stone through glass, momentum carrying me through the white doorway. It was open and ready to devour me.

RED. No matter what direction I looked, the color tinted my vision, flowing in cords of varying degrees of opacity like impenetrable waves.

Blood, that's what it was, the smell of iron thick in my nostrils. I couldn't shake it. I knew she was there if only I could—

Fly me away...

The song pierced the silence like a gunshot in the wilderness, my body seizing like the hunted deer, alert and ready to flee.

"Mona, Mona!"

Like the first time, I tried to speak, but no sound came out. I needed her to hear me, to know I'd come back for her.

A single eye reflected at me in the shattered rearview mirror, the cracks multiplying it into a collection of grotesque cyclops, each eye embedded in a sea of ichor. A glob of red rolled down my right eye, an avalanche clearing a path I could finally see through.

From this cold, dark place...

Ragged inhalations. Crashing waves. Mona's final song. I could hardly see my surroundings, but I could hear her suffering, her whimpers, escaping her body—my body—and the horrific gurgling of fluid choking off her limited air supply, the smell of gasoline smothering.

"Mona! I'm right here. I'm going to figure out how to save you. I— I can do it."

The convulsion hit like a shock to the chest, her whole body spasming against the seatbelt. The world opened up then, the blood washing away to reveal the interior of the car, shattered glass sparkling on the roof above like the starry night sky.

I tried to control the eye to assess her injuries, but I was overruled, our focal point recentering on the rearview mirror as she, or maybe destiny itself, manhandled me into obedience.

She looked like something out of a horror story, and my mind was unable to comprehend the extent of the damage done to her. It hadn't been this bad the last time; now her injuries were even more severe.

Mona opened her mouth, lips moving as if to speak, and she spasmed again, a stream of blood erupting to cover the mirror. I wanted to close my eyes, to banish seeing her this way, but I wasn't in the driver's seat of her body. That single eye remained opened, unable to blink, taking in its own end.

A bright escape...

That voice hung in the air, prolonged like a piano key with the sustain pedal depressed.

It's time to change my fate, today...

Something stabbed me, a heat that warmed my belly rather than an intense penetration, and began to pull. The intensity accelerated, my body beginning to fold itself inside out while my outer self was sucked into my navel like a bubble being blown out of a bubble wand in reverse.

The world warped, and with a loud boom, I returned to darkness.

LIGHT, pure and intense, shattered my sense of equilibrium. Up became down and left became right before flipping its orientation. Gravity had no place where I'd gone, only weightlessness.

Trrreeeee...

A long, drawn-out death rattle wormed its way into my ears from every direction. That final breath uttered at her end.

Vvvvoooorrrrr.

I sat up, my ears ringing with Mona's otherworldly song and mouth filled with the repulsive taste of vomit, the visual representation of its ejection on display in a Jackson Pollock fresco of partially digested pizza in front of me.

My mind raced to process the influx of stimuli bombarding my brain, leading to another test of my gag reflex. My olfactory receptors finally caught up and rejected the scent.

"What the hell happened?"

I struggled to my feet and got a glass of water from the kitchen.

Mona. I'd seen her again, but just the end, her eyes trying to convey a message to me. She implored something, didn't she?

That first time at her funeral, I knew she sensed me in the reflection of the mirror. It wasn't as definitive this time, but I swear she knew I was there. I recognized her cues better than anyone, but what was it?

A collage of memories flickered in my mind, her eyes wide and intense on me whenever she wanted me to think.

"I love you, Trev, but you are the smartest and, sometimes, the dumbest man I know. Think about it."

If she could just jibe me one more time...

The refrigerator was covered in magnets, each holding a picture of Mona: our wedding day, a day at the beach with friends, and her in an elegant gown, gray eyes piercing, burrowing to my core.

I shivered and let my head sink, a posture of defeat, my gaze trailing down the stainless-steel backdrop, and there, on the edge at counter height, was a piece of newspaper, so different from the glossy high-definition photos.

Monaciel Amato-Pierre, age 31, formerly of Carmel Highlands, passed away Thursday. She is survived by her husband, mother, father, and sister.

My heart skipped a beat, the obituary slicing me like the rusty knife that leaves an infected laceration. I felt it all over again, the weight on my shoulders, my stomach's free fall, my sapped strength as my knees gave way... I was right back there in the funeral home.

My tailbone landed roughly against the countertop as I slid to the floor.

"She is survived by her husband...," I whispered.

Was she even really gone? I hadn't seen her body after she passed; I couldn't bring myself to do it. And then, at the funeral, I was transported to the moment of her death. That had to be for a reason. What if I could really save her?

"How do you propose to do that, you idiot? Smartest and dumbest man alive," I chided myself.

If only I could figure out what she was trying to tell me, then maybe I'd have some clue. If I could just see it again from the beginning, like in—

That was it. It finally dawned on me. I needed to be with Mona again. Not just spiritually seeking her, but physically.

That whole time, I'd been trying to reach her through the music but from a distance. Proximity mattered, like at the funeral when I first went through the white door in the very place she was physically supposed to be.

There *had* been recognition in her eyes then. I know I wasn't mistaken. That had to be the key.

I changed my clothes, grabbed my phone on my way out the door, and got into my car for the first time since the police called me the night of her accident. I was going to her grave.

THE AIR WAS cool and salty, and the thick California coastal fog hung over the headstones as I wandered the vast maze. It was late afternoon, but I couldn't tell. The thick gray air hindered my visibility and slowed my pace to careful, deliberate steps. My shoulders were hunched as I moved, walking like a lost traveler in the desert seeking an oasis.

Name after name crossed my wandering gaze as I passed each tombstone, desperate to find Mona's grave unobserved. I was keenly aware that I was in the midst of a cemetery during the day, no matter how foggy it was. When I found Mona, nothing would stop me from proceeding, but I didn't need any bystanders present to complicate the situation. I was here to reach Mona's coffin and, just like at her funeral, enter that white doorway right at the source, where her body was supposed to be.

Suddenly, a pulse rippled through the air, letting me know I was getting close. I'd felt it before. It was Mona's presence; that beat, like that of her heart. It was palpable.

Lub-dub.

I heard a snap and pivoted sharply to my left. The gnarled tree, that same one that Mona and I made love beneath for the first time, loomed over me, its thick, interlaced branches reaching down to trap me in its embrace. I clenched my eyes, bracing myself for contact.

Nothing happened. The tree stood tall and still as it always had, standing guard over its deceased charges.

Taking a breath, I let my feet carry me forward, my body on autopilot, zeroing in on that beat in the air like an enemy aircraft on radar, the blips growing more pronounced the closer I got.

Lub-dub.

The air stilled, and it took me a moment to realize I wasn't moving. In the foreground was a strip of freshly turned soil covered in wilted flowers, conspicuous for its lack of headstone.

"Mona, I'm here…"

I took a cursory glance from side to side to ensure I was alone before I plunged my hands into the soil. I could feel the electricity there. My fingers tingled as the static coursed up my arms, leaving them riddled with gooseflesh. She was really there, the thumping of her heart presaging each shock, beckoning me like Poe's Tell-Tale Heart.

Lub-dub. Lub-dub. Lub-dub.

"Mona!"

I started to dig, slowly at first, then more quickly with each jolt, the dirt and small stones burrowing under my fingernails and scraping my knuckles. I was like a backhoe conducting an excavation, my hands clawing deep and scooping the dirt out toward me.

Lub-dub. Lub-dub. Lub-dub.

The soil mingled with the mist spiraling around me, tinting the world from gray to brown, causing rivulets of dirty sweat to paint my face. I needed to reach that doorway; Mona was there waiting for me.

"I'm coming! Don't worry, I'm coming," I whispered, repeating it again and again like a chant, trying to reassure her as much as myself. I wondered how I was going to pierce the resistance that prevented me from helping her and remove her from that place, but my wandering thoughts were soon drowned out by the *lub-dub* that was growing ever louder.

My arms grew weary as minutes passed, my own heart ricocheting against my ribs like a heated racquetball tournament inside my chest. I slowed, flailing about in my desperation. My thumbnail cracked as a pebble drove under it, pealing it away from hyponychium and exposing the nail bed. I screamed, grabbing my finger and trying to staunch the blood, streams of it sluicing out from my grasp.

I couldn't continue. I'd come so close, but looking at the small indentation I'd made, I realized I was no closer than a child in a sandbox trying to dig to the center of the Earth, my efforts feeling no less futile.

The music had led me to her, connected me to her, but I'd failed to bring her out of the grave to which she didn't belong.

"Mona, I—I'm so sorry—" I said, my throat tight as I choked back tears.

Every step forward, I took three steps back, reliving the devastation of my initial loss with every failure to reach her.

I could no longer feel her, the *lub-dub* growing silent.

I screamed, my voice swallowed by the foggy emptiness as I lost consciousness.

Bzzt, Bzzt.

I opened my eyes, and Mona's gravestone was horizontal before me. When had I lay down?

I rubbed the clumped dirt from my cheek as I sat up and assessed my mangled thumb in the waning twilight. It was black with dried mud and coagulated blood. It was an infection waiting to happen.

Bzzt, Bzzt.

Oh, that's what had awoken me, I thought as I took my phone out of my pocket. Bre.

> BRE
> 5:58 PM
>
> Haven't heard from you. Did you try it?
>
> 6:01 PM
>
> ok, please answer. I'm dying over here!

I'd completely forgotten to let her know about the sound healing. Bre had come up with the idea and I'd left her hanging. But what could she do? Only I could go through the doorway to get Mona. No, Bre couldn't help me any further.

6:03 PM

Sorry, not much different than before. I had the idea to try again at the cemetery since that's where this all started. Communing with her and all that. I'll keep you posted.

And thanks.

Her response was immediate, coming in faster than my finger could shut off the phone's screen.

6:04 PM

OMG wtf? I'm coming.

That was not the response I expected, but I should have known better. I couldn't have her here distracting me. I had to do this alone.

I started to type something to that effect, but before I could send it off, she beat me to the punch.

6:04 PM

Don't argue. I'm ignoring anything you have to say until I see you...

I sighed, a loud whoosh in the silence. I'd better get started.

I WENT through the steps I had at home, playing the sound healing playlist before switching to Gigi McLean. The process happened even more quickly, the sensations as powerful as touching a live wire, my body vibrating painfully.

I swooped down from a bird's-eye view, crashing into Mona's mind like a kamikaze pilot. We peered up at the rearview mirror: no cracks in it or in her body. The accident hadn't happened yet. She trembled, bringing her hand to grasp her chest for a moment.

"Where did that cold chill come from?" Mona asked aloud,

rubbing her right hand along the goose bumps on her opposite arm before reaching out to turn up the heat.

That was new. The scene was already different from the first time, but there was something about the cold chill—had I done that to her? Was that a sign I could finally reach her?

Fly me away. From this cold, dark place...

A bright escape. It's time to change my fate, today...

Returning her hand to the steering wheel so she was once again driving ten and two, Mona began tapping against the chilled leather as the song picked up pace. This was it.

I couldn't yell or scream, but she felt me connect with her. What if I...

I pushed then, not physically, but mentally, throwing all of my love and my grief into our collective sense of being, imploring her to feel me there with her.

More goose bumps bloomed along her arms, and she adjusted the heating vents to include the ones built into the dash, not just those for her feet. Her eyes looked down for just that split second to adjust her comfort as the erratic swerve of the approaching head-lights presaged the event I hoped to stop.

It hadn't been enough.

I studied her face, those gray eyes, dark blonde hair, and that small mole above her lip line on the left side. All that I'd fallen in love with, unaware of the guided missile veering off its course with her in its crosshairs.

Mona's headlights lit up the exit sign, and her gaze drifted up to read it, oblivious to the danger that was advancing on her. I felt a warmth inside her, that radiant sensation of home and safety.

Goddamit, she'd almost made it home to me. But I was here now if I could only get her to stop.

As I deliberated, wondering how I could get Mona to hear my pleas, lights flared into being in front of her, eradicating all dark-ness like the flash of a lightning strike. Her eyes widened in surprise and fear. She tried to spring into action, but her hands moved as though she were underwater, her subtle movements having no discernible effect on the outcome of the storm raging on the surface.

The world spun. Stars and then darkness, stars, dark, stars, dark, again and again at an ever-increasing rate until a faint halo of light became the only visual reality.

Mona's eyes twitched, infinitesimally, but enough for us to see a new vision.

It was the night of our rehearsal dinner, and Mona looked at me, her eyes not leaving mine for a long time. I wasn't sure what she saw on my face, but there was a flutter of her eyelids, a tell of knowing before she blinked her eyes closed, keeping them that way just a bit longer than normal, an acceptance.

"No—"

Sound returned with a vengeance; a symphony of destruction, like hearing the death of a star, erupted around us. The airbags deployed as the car hit the rocky shore far below the road, completing its revolution to finish upside down, a jagged spire piercing the passenger seat and sending fragments of the center console into Mona's arm, strips of flesh and sinew tearing away from her to dangle like a piece of hanging beef in an aging room.

Everything was hazy, a roaring static blurring everything in hues of gray, white, and black. I couldn't focus, and silhouettes of the tangible became lost in the murk, the stench of gasoline nearly suffocating.

Mona! Baby, where are you?

She'd never been able to hear my thoughts before, but I had to try as I flailed in the void. The static stuttered, a visible ripple that flowed out into the distance like a rope of tactile sound I could use to climb back to her, the safety rope in the blizzard.

Reaching out, I closed my fingers around it and—

Mona opened her eyes, no, just a single eye, as one refused to open, and the realization of what had just occurred caught up with her. Red, the red of blood—her blood—covered everything.

It was on her hands, the steering wheel, and her face. She shifted her gaze to the rearview mirror and caught her reflection: one eye was fused shut by a shard of glass that had speared it, and tiny droplets dripped out at regular intervals.

She opened her mouth to speak or scream, I had no idea which, and spat out a glob of blood that made a splashing noise as it hit the ever-growing puddle accumulating on the roof, her hair brushing against it like the fine bristles of a paintbrush.

I was paralyzed, seeing what she saw; the fear evident on her face chilled me to my core. She knew that there was no hope. She understood that she would die.

Her single eye became frantic as it seemed to search for something in the shattered rearview mirror, the reflection of eight eyes staring back and darting from side to side. Suddenly, her eye stopped looking back at the bloody ruin of herself, but with its intensity, I knew she had found what she sought. Mona found me.

"Trreee—"

Her voice broke off with the garble of blood rushing down her esophagus before being punctuated with a long wheeze.

Fly me away...

I gasped as I returned to the cemetery, the song having ended on my phone. My arms shivered as the cold breeze brushed against the thin sheen of sweat covering my arms and face.

That wasn't how it happened the last time I saw it; it was different. This time, the scene had been so much more gruesome, and to feel her resignation to the fate she'd been dealt...

Had I done that? Did Mona get dealt an even more torturous blow because she felt me there with her, almost as if I altered the past?

"I need to go back," I whispered aloud, more to affirm my solidity and sense of agency than anything else.

I crawled to the top of Mona's burial plot and rolled over onto my back to alleviate some of my fatigue, unable to sit upright any longer.

"Sorry about the flowers," I said, feeling them smash beneath my weight.

Unlocking my phone, I clicked on Gigi McLean again and pressed play. The gap was bridged; I could reach Mona now, like the first time, but my job wasn't done. I had to push it a step further, again and again if I had to, in order to give her that nudge that would stop the accident. Whether Mona slammed on the brakes and stopped before the driver could hit her or she swerved out of the way entirely, I didn't know, but I'd find something.

I knew the physical doorway was likely the key, but with my limbs still sapped of strength, I needed to try what I could before digging any further.

I closed my eyes and reentered my worst nightmare as the opening lyrics of Gigi McLean began.

REENTRY BECAME EASIER the more I did it with the link between me and the spirit world firmly in place. As soon as I heard that opening verse, *Fly me away...,* I returned to Mona, crashing into her more forcefully than the time preceding.

Over and over again, I tried to sway events, launching my consciousness, my essence, against her, willing her to stop and see what was coming for her, but every time, she brushed it off as a chill —the crossing of paths with a spirit taking a stroll on the long road.

"Mona, listen!" I tried to scream at her, but I knew it was folly, and she couldn't hear me. While I was with her, living her experience through her eyes, I didn't have control of the wheel. I was destined to relive this misery from the driver's seat with everything around me on autopilot. If only the experience didn't tear a bit more of my soul each time I did it.

It would be one thing to see the same scene on repeat, but instead, each time I re-experienced it, her death grew more unspeakable, more grisly.

At first, it had been her damaged eye, changing from being a piece of glass piercing it closed to the entire thing being ripped from her face, the glass still wedged in the socket while the eye bathed in the pool of blood on the car's ceiling, completely severed from her body.

Then it was the glass, more and more shards embedding themselves into her cheeks and hands until she began to shimmer like the diamond on her finger, droplets of blood coloring her exposed skin to eradicate any semblance of who she was.

The worst, though, was her throat. She tried to call my name, spitting up blood in the process and not quite being able to formulate words. With each visit, her articulation deteriorated until the glass shards, springing up all over her exposed skin, became a giant fragment of the windshield, nearly severing her neck, her final moments of lucidity being nothing more than a death rattle, her single eye affixed on me accusingly while the air became unbreathable with the stench of gasoline and burning oil.

After each time her death concluded, I was ejected back to reality, prostrate in the dirt, pleading for her forgiveness that I couldn't end the pain. I felt confident that if I just went one more time, that would be the time I'd save her; that on that next visit, I would get her to stop the car, and I'd awake with her next to me.

I looked for any excuse to return, like a junky to his favorite drug, ignoring the fact that each time I did, I watched her suffer more than ever before. I knew it had to be because of me, messing with the spirit world where those who are living shouldn't venture, but why was I transferred there in the first place unless it was to help her? It felt like a losing battle; my initial elation at seeing her hands when I arrived always deteriorated to desperation as I raced against the clock to witness her ever-worsening end.

"Trevor."

A whisper in the wind. I lifted my head from the dirt, whipping my head from side to side. She was here!

"Mona!"

I got to my knees.

"Mona!"

"Trevor," the voice became louder, approaching me, "it's Bre. What are you doing on the ground?"

I stood, turning to face her. I should have known it was too good to be true.

"You didn't need to come," I told her, patting the dirt off my pants.

"Yes, I did, first of all, and second, what the hell happened to your thumb and—" She cut off, her eyes assessing me before lowering to the small hole I dug with my hands.

She took a step back.

"What's going on here, Trev?"

I sighed. Bre was my last ally, the only one who seemed to believe I could reach my wife, but her expression conveyed that her allegiance was faltering.

"I told you, I've communed with her. I've revisited her so many times since we texted."

Bre crossed her arms, rubbing them as if fighting a chill. We'd always been close, Mona telling me that if anything ever happened to her, I'd be in good hands, but for the first time, Bre looked at me like a stranger.

"I don't know how that is supposed to work, Trev, but I texted you about thirty minutes ago. How many times could this have happened in that time?"

I opened my mouth, but no words came out. I'd been ejected and reentered, replaying the scene repeatedly, like a child with their favorite movie, at least twenty times. Despite all of that, I was back at square one. Now that Bre was here, I had to make her realize that I needed her help to finally save Mona. We had to dig up her coffin so that I could reach the doorway inside of it. It was clear to me now that it was truly the only way; anything else would just be torture to Mona.

I swallowed and tried again to speak.

"At least a dozen," I shrugged, as if it was the most common thing in the world, before continuing, "but, Bre, she's hurting. Every time I return, it's worse than the time before it. I have to break that cycle."

Bre stared at me, eyes blank. I pressed on.

"At her funeral, I saw a doorway come out of her coffin. I've seen it a few other times in my mind, but I felt the most strongly with her, almost as if I could communicate with her, when I was able to physically go through that door. That's how I save her. I need to go through that door again at the source. Which means we need access to her coffin. I—"

Bre slapped her hands against her legs and stomped her foot.

"Have you lost your fucking mind? We aren't digging up my sister! I—Look, I get your world has been destroyed; mine has too, but, Trevor, what the hell is going on? I was with you up to this point. I believe in sound healing, that's why I mentioned it to you, and in spirits, too; I really do. I feel like she's always talking to me, but digging her up?"

Bre turned away from me, clutching her hands to her breast.

"Even I know that is something you don't mess with. If this is where we've gotten to... we need to leave her be," her voice faltered at the last. Her head swiveled to face me again, and tears welled up, ready for release.

I let my head hang, not because I thought she was right but because I felt shame for causing her pain. Unfortunately, she was wrong, and I'd show her.

"You don't need to help me. I'll do this on my own," I said.

She looked stricken, as though the thought that I would continue had never crossed her mind. Bre thought she could dissuade me.

"I... Trevor." Bre paused, unsure of how to continue.

We just looked at each other, unsure how to communicate for the first time. I could see the struggle on her face, the shifting emotions, as she tried to figure out how we'd get past this, but ultimately, she just looked away in resignation.

I cleared my throat.

"Bre—" She faced me and held up her hand.

"Just go back to your house tonight and sleep on it. Can you do that for me?"

I sighed. "Sure, Bre. I can do that."

The tension melted away as her shoulders loosened, lowering away from her ears. She flicked her hand at my thumb.

"Also, you need to have that looked at."

I smirked.

"Yeah, yeah, I know."

I put my arm around her, and she flinched but didn't push me away. She was trying. We had too much history together not to make an effort.

We walked back to our cars, and I felt a pang of regret, knowing that I'd lied to her. I would go home, but I didn't plan on waiting until morning to return. I just needed a shovel, and then I would come back. Mona was waiting for me.

———

THE CEMETERY WAS much as it was during the day, quiet and misty, the roiling plumes of condensation twirling around me like wraiths, ominous and full of malicious intent. The darkness brought with it new sensations as though the other spirits were alive and watchful, joining Mona in their vigil. I could sense her there with me.

As soon as I'd gotten home, I could feel her beckoning me to return, to save her from the eternal torment. I packed diligently, grabbing a shovel, a lantern, and warm clothes, knowing I wouldn't return for a while. I was on the cusp of an odyssey, and I had no idea if it would last a fraction of a second or span forty days and nights like those Jesus spent in the desert.

Thunkt.

The shovel slid into the dirt without resistance, the damp soil parting around it like a serving spoon in a Jell-O mold.

One scoop.

Two scoops.

Three scoops.

I moved with the intensity of a man with nothing to lose, as if the devil himself were breathing down my neck. I would not be denied; I would reach that white door. Yet Bre was nestled in the back of my consciousness, an unwelcome companion reminding me of my betrayal.

There was really no choice between her and my wife, but I knew she wouldn't understand with Mona having passed. I felt I owed her some explanation, but what could I say? I agreed to something, and then I took it back. After I found the door, stopped the accident, and pulled Mona back through with me, she'd be an idiot not to admit her mistake.

Three feet.

My rectangle expanded to include the entire footprint of the already-turned earth, walls of soil forming around me like a minia-ture Grand Canyon. Just a few feet more to go.

I was sweating, my heart racing.

I distracted myself with the next step in the process, the doorway. Would it be the same? How would I get Mona back out? While I saw the door when I entered, I never saw it when I was ejected from her body. I'd been yanked out, manhandled, and discarded, and only saw it afterward at her funeral once I was back in reality as it towered before me. But what about when I was a part of Mona? What exit did I look for?

I took few breaks as my arms became numb with fatigue. The moment I stopped before reaching her coffin would be the moment I was defeated. I knew myself. I knew my limitations. Luckily, this cemetery had no security, as that type of interruption would have been game over.

Clang.

I'd struck something. Euphoria flooded my system as I cleared the dirt to reveal shiny gunmetal—the lid. I only needed enough clear space for the top to open, and I'd be home free. I increased my pace, hardly able to lift the shovel anymore but refusing to give up.

After two more scoops, the shovel fell from my hands as I was unable to hold it up any longer. My arms were on fire so I began kicking dirt away in giant thrusts. I was so close...

"Yes," I yelled as my feet exposed enough room for a handhold, and plunging my hands into the final layer of dirt around the side handle, I yanked the top open.

It was my final moment before the point of no return. I'd dreamt of it for weeks, that moment when I could reach into that other place and whisk Mona away before the other car could find her, but a part of me, a rational seed being smothered by the weeds of delusion, desired for me to see nothing but her body at rest, to finally put this unachievable hell to bed. That isn't what I found. Instead, there was blackness so thick that it dulled the rays of sunlight trying to peek over the horizon, grabbing them and pulling them down into their nothingness.

Where was the doorway? It had to be there. I squinted, trying to see what lay in the coffin, but the dark was too absolute.

"Mona! Mona!"

My words were swallowed, gulped down like a hair in a drain, a ripple in the blackness that had no hope of reversing course.

Eevvvoorrr.

It was faint and hollow, like yelling into a massive hangar and only hearing the remnants of the echo on the other side.

Rrreeevvooor.

Trevor. She's calling me.

And that was it, the moment rationality was banished. I lunged forward, throwing myself into the incorporeal maw.

Flash.

When the priest finished making the sign of the cross, I held up my quivering hand as if I were a boy back in Sunday school, only this time I was seeking permission for something I was in complete control of. The eyes of dozens of onlookers pivoted to me, my hand a beacon, the lighthouse in the fog signaling all ships in peril to my harbor for safety. Except I wasn't a haven but a harbinger of something more perilous.

"Father, I know this is unorthodox, but... I need to see Mona."

The faces in the crowd ranged from concern to tearful bewilderment. Opening a casket before it's about to be buried is highly unusual.

"Trevor, my son. I don't think—"

I grabbed his cassock, surprised at my ferocity. The priest's eyes widened. It was a move of desperation, not intimidation, but my actions had the latter effect as my knuckles turned white with the force of my grip.

The priest cleared his throat and patted my hands, a bead of sweat dripping down his brow.

"As you wish."

I could feel my arms shaking like I'd had too much Redbull; pulses of electricity were coursing through my fingers. I needed to calm down. Mona needed to know I could be her Trevor without her, a man who could live a life as a soloist after the duet's final show.

I began to hum our song, that melody of peace we played when we needed to escape.

Fly me away...

I released the priest's garb, lowering my eyes in repentance as he lifted the cover of the casket.

Mona's parents stepped forward quickly, their umbrellas raised to prevent her body from getting wet, all the while staring at me as though I'd lost touch with my senses.

Her father mumbled; I assumed he was meaning to curse me for my disrespect or something close to it, but Bre grabbed his arm, her eyes menacing.

I nodded to her appreciatively, took a deep breath, and stepped up to the casket's side.

Flash.

"DARLING! We were talking about your husband-to-be's writing."

"What about it?"

Her father's eyes had narrowed at her tone.

"Honey, listen—"

"No, Dad, you listen. I'm not having this, especially the night before our wedding, and that's final."

She pulled me away from the table, my face beaming with triumph.

"I'm so sorry," she started, but I stopped her with a kiss.

"Honey, it's fine. Let's enjoy our night."

I embraced her then, feeling the warmth of her body against mine, that sense of wholeness she always filled me with.

We stood that way for several moments, the opening verses of our favorite song playing faintly in the background.

Fly me away...

Mona leaned back from me, looking into my eyes and holding my gaze. I wasn't sure what she'd seen on my face, but there was something there, the way her brows scrunched. She recognized something; had it been doubt?

She nodded, a slight bob of the head that I almost didn't register.

"You okay?" I asked.

Lifting her hand and brushing my hair back into place, she just smiled, her eyes full of acceptance and, what was it, sadness?

"All is good. I love you, Trev."

She kissed me on the lips while Gigi McLean continued to sing.

It's time to change my fate, today...

FLASH.

MONA GRABBED my hand as I continued to fidget, moving it in a gentle *rat-a-tat-tat* motion and saying, "We always have the music in us."

She always knew what to say when I'd get into one of my moods. Despite being a writer and needing my silence to create, whenever my brain hit a snag that exposed my consciousness to the world at large, I'd recoil into a whirlwind of anxiety. The wilderness helped her recenter herself as she listened to nature's symphony. It began to do the same for me as long as I had her there to show me the way.

"It's so humbling being out here, isn't it? Away from the city and just listening to the woods. It's spiritual."

The stars were just beginning to shine through the blue sky as it transitioned to twilight. I turned my head from our open-topped tent to look at her profile, the scent of her shampoo wafting into my nose, filling me with the comfort of home in the gentle breeze.

"It's awfully quiet, that's for sure."

"Ugh, Trev, come on. There is so much around us if you just open up your mind. Listen to the wind; you can hear the whispers."

"Whispers?"

"Of those that came before us."

I shivered from a sudden caress of cold. It was like another presence crossed my path.

"There's something."

She grabbed my hand and gave it a squeeze, her warmth shattering the icy spike of fear I felt slithering through me.

Our eyes met.

"Fly me away," she started.

"From this cold, dark place," we sang together, the sun's last light extinguishing behind the western horizon.

FLASH, *flash, flash.*

THE FRAME of a doorway whizzed past me before depositing me into the dark open air. The sky erupted with the crackling of lightning all around me as thunder boomed instantaneously.

Moments before, I'd been struggling to peer into the dark depths of Mona's coffin before throwing caution to the wind and diving into it. My gamble paid off. The doorway was there, and I was now through it, wholly in my own form and body, instead of being a wraith behind Mona's eyes. I'd pierced the fourth wall.

My head throbbed as the memories coalesced, clear as day, in my mind. There'd been so much I'd forgotten, the connections that led me to that moment finally complete.

Our song had always been there, Gigi McLean, the lodestone drawing the puzzle pieces of our life together to form our fate. As long as I followed Gigi's words, those lyrics would draw me back to

Mona. They brought me back to her, and through them, Mona intended me to save her; I just knew it.

I pulled my limbs against my sides, making my body into a rocket to increase my speed like an action star in a movie, as I plummeted toward her car curving along SR 1 on the California coast. Flipping my legs forward, I braced myself for impact and slowed to float down into the passenger seat like a feather, pivoting to and fro toward the ground.

I landed with a soft thud and released my breath, shocked that my hands were steady after plunging thousands of feet.

Fly me away...

The song had started, and a glint in the corner of my eye caught my attention. Mona's diamond ring dazzled in the car's faint overhead glow on her hand perched atop the steering wheel while the other turned the volume dial up before shifting to the heat, cranking it to bask our feet with sauna-like intensity.

I'd always complained or rolled my eyes at how cold she was, me suffering through the house being kept at seventy-six degrees for her sake; I'd do anything for her, and at that moment, I didn't care. Hell, I welcomed it.

Mona, my love, my everything, was right next to me, a smile wide on her face as Gigi McLean serenaded us like on so many other nights.

We always have the music in us. Yes, we did, Mona, baby, yes, we did. I let my head fall back and laughed, a rich noise of joy I hadn't felt in the better part of a month resounding in my ears. Oh God, how good it felt to finally let all the sorrow go.

Wiping a tear from my eye, I rested my head on the headrest and glanced over at her.

"I love you," I said.

There was no response as she brushed her fingers through her hair, but she looked so happy, her smile wide and her eyes crinkling ever so slightly at the edges.

I reached my hand out, needing to touch her one more time, but my fingers passed right through her, like walking through the images of a projector on a screen.

My smile faded. Lights flashed quickly in the distance.

"No," I whispered, looking forward before pivoting to Mona and then back again.

"No, no, no. Not again. I can't again. I'm here this time. I'm here. Mona! I'm here!"

Lub-dub. Lub-dub. Lub-dub.

My heart was beating faster and faster, a drum in my chest calling my nerves to war. I had come all this way to stop this, and nothing was different. I dug up her grave and went through the doorway. I was sitting next to her! Why wasn't it different?

"Mona! Mona, please, goddamit!"

I was pleading, but she couldn't hear me. Her eyes shifted for just a second at that pivotal moment after the car came around the bend, its tires squealing as it lost control.

"Mona!"

I slammed my hand down, channeling all my love, sorrow, regrets, and guilt into a bludgeon of hope that this time it could be different, that I could save her.

Time slowed as I made contact with her arm, releasing a jolt of intense heat that scorched my hand, like grabbing a hot iron off the ironing board. Mona's eyes widened, her head pivoted slowly in my direction, and her hair floated outward like an astronaut in space.

Shock played across her features before her eyes narrowed in recognition. She glowed like an angel, a halo around her body as her lips started to move.

"Trevor."

Her words were in slow motion, a movie being played back at 1/10 speed.

I opened my mouth to reply, to tell her I'd come for her as I promised, that everything would be okay, but the lights got brighter.

Normal speed returned.

The sound ceased, or maybe the cacophony was so great I could no longer discern the difference between auditory pandemonium and silence.

I flew into the passenger door, my gaze never leaving Mona. She was thrown about like a rag doll, a chew toy in the mouth of a dog on a mission of destruction. The car became airborne, shards of glass floating like constellations as we orbited around them, the car somersaulting through the air to the rocky shoreline below.

The windows were shattered, their pieces scratching and embedding themselves into Mona's face, neck, and hands. The driver's-side armrest had broken off and curled into her side, leaving her arm a mangled piece of flesh that dangled from strands of muscle and sinew. It was pure horror.

"Mona!"

We continued our fall with the rocks fast approaching.

I reached for her, wanting her to know I'd be going with her this time. If I couldn't save her, at least I wouldn't let her leave this world alone.

My fingers swung at open air, unable to reach her; it was like reaching for the edge of a cliff from below, my arm not quite long enough to grasp the ledge.

Using every ounce of my strength, I battled the centrifugal force and lunged forward, brushing her hair away from her face. My stomach dropped as our eyes met, that feeling of my world collapsing. I was faced with a mask of blood, her eyes locked onto mine with that look of knowing, of recognition, the same one she'd given me at our rehearsal dinner.

She saw me. Mona knew I was there, but I'd failed her.

Crash.

The sound of ripping and mangled metal fractured our final moment together as we hit the bottom of our descent, a jagged spire of stone piercing the car's roof and impaling Mona in the chest while glass filleted her face. Blood splattered me, blotting out my view as the chaos settled into stillness.

I gasped, realizing I could still breathe, the scent of gasoline wafting into my nostrils. I wiped the blood from my eyes, lifting the red veil, and retched. My wife, my love, stared back at me. There was nothing left of her; the right side of her face was sliced cleanly off by a sizable chunk of the windshield, and her last whisper of life escaped the gaping hole in her trachea.

Fly me away...

"Nooooo—" I screamed, and, like so many times before, everything went black.

THERE WAS A SUCKING SOUND, like water whirlpooling down a drain, before I was pulled out of the doorway and tossed out into the morning light, my back slamming into the dirt wall surrounding her exposed coffin.

Vertigo twisted my sense of orientation as I tried to recalibrate my reality. I'd been there with Mona. She'd been within my grasp, and I'd failed. Our whole relationship, I'd feared letting her down, doing something that would drive her away, leaving me alone again, that wound from my mother's death festering and poisoning my perspective of what my life with Mona could bring. It started almost immediately.

The first time I'd met her, something deep inside of me started to sing and synchronize, a great harmonizing of music I couldn't see but could feel picking up her rhythm and forming its own a cappella. It was love at first sight, and I was terrified.

Each time I saw her after, every single encounter, I waited for the shoe to drop where she'd exit my life, leaving me alone with my jazz, a medium that transformed from my guiding light to just another part of my life with Mona. If she went, I'd be left with only silence and the black nothingness of my childhood. For some crazy reason, she'd stayed.

We had money struggles, my battles with her father, and occasionally bouts of melancholy instigated by my feelings of inadequacy. Despite it all, we endured, our love more powerful than anything I ever thought possible.

I should have been reassured, but no, my fear never abated. In my bones, I never thought we'd last; after all, our lives are finite. And at the end of it all, Mona had been taken from me. And then I'd had a chance to undo it, but I'd blown it.

A cloud of dust swirled as the wind spiraled into our hole six feet under, stinging my eyes and blurring my vision. I held up my hand, trying to see inside the open half of her coffin. Maybe I could try again?

When the dust finally started to clear—it had been as thick as a sandstorm just moments before—I watched as the remnants of the charred doorway crumbled into minuscule particles, blowing away in the breeze and with it, as though a shroud had been lifted, any further illusion as I saw Mona below me, bloody gashes across her arms, neck, and face, a gaping hole being the only remnant of one side of her face, the side I'd seen the piece of glass penetrate.

I recoiled, returning to where I'd been moments before, planted against the earthen wall. She hadn't been there, I could've sworn, and those wounds...

I've heard people describe the moment they've finally come to terms with the death of a loved one, and I don't know how they even found words to articulate it. My heartbreak was too immense, and the feeling that my insides were ripped from my body was too gruesome. Simply put, I felt lost and empty, like a rudderless boat being washed away to the ends of the Earth and hoping it was flat so I could plunge off the edge to my demise.

I buried my head in my hands, stifling the screams I wanted to unleash. I'd reached the end. I felt vomit burn my throat, but I held it down.

"Jesus Christ!"

I looked up.

John stood above me, Dan and Bre on either side of him. Their eyes were filled with horror, except for Mona's father; his gaze was only filled with rage.

"What have you done to her? Get away from her right now!"

I opened my mouth to protest, but I couldn't produce any sound.

Any fight I'd had evaporated when my mind finally registered her body. I hadn't seen Mona after the accident; her family had helped with that as I'd been too bereft to deal with it, but I knew she shouldn't look how she does now, blood painting her body and seeping from fresh wounds, as though the accident had just happened rather than weeks before. All of those slashes and cuts, I'd just seen them made. How had I been so stupid? Mona died weeks ago, but my obsession killed her dozens more times. She suffered again and again because of me.

"Trev, give me your hand."

It was Dan. He'd moved closer, reaching down to help me out. I stared at him, unable to move.

"Get out of there right now, Trevor! So help me, God. You'll pay for this," John screamed at me, snapping me out of my daze. His hands were in the air, gesticulating wildly.

It would have been comical if his actions hadn't been warranted. I tortured his daughter.

I stood, thrust out my hand to grab Dan's, and heard Bre gasp. Dan looked away and clutched it firmly, sending searing pain down my arm. My knees buckled.

It took me a moment to remember why the hand that Dan was hauling me up by was a blackened ruin, the memory flashing through my head with an intensity that left me faint.

Time slowed as I made contact with her arm, releasing a jolt of intense heat that scorched my hand like grabbing a hot iron off the ironing board.

I'd touched Mona a final time, and my trespass earned me a scar for going where I didn't belong.

"Aaaaahhhh," I howled as Dan hoisted me up, accompanying pairs of hands assisted in grabbing me and depositing me on the ground.

I lost focus; I may have blacked out from the pain, but I can't quite remember. Voices circled me. Murmurs in various pitches until I homed in on one beside my ear.

"I'm sorry, Trev, I didn't want to do this, but I warned you. You were acting crazy the other night, and after you threw us out, I called and texted. I begged you to talk to someone and get help, but you didn't have the decency to respond. I didn't know what else to do, especially after Bre told us you would do this."

My eyes refocused on Dan's face above me, his pale green eyes downcast. He'd always been a friend trying to do the right thing, and with all my ups and downs, he was right there making sure I had somewhere to turn when I didn't want to burden Mona. How did I repay him? Instead of trying to see reason, or at least reality from his point of view, I treated him like garbage.

He may not have believed that I could see Mona, but he was right to demand I stop.

"Officers, arrest him. Look what he's done."

I could see John glowering at me off to the right, motioning to the police officers, four of them in full uniform, to apprehend me.

"He clearly is having a dissociative break. I've consulted a therapist and my attorney about this. I'm pressing charges and want him admitted."

One of the officers faced John, hands up disarmingly, trying to deescalate his anger.

"We understand, sir, but we need you to calm down and let us handle this, okay?"

John threw his hands up, and Bre grabbed his arm, leading him to the side. She wouldn't look at me. Bre had known I would break my word. I didn't blame her for telling them my plan.

"Bre," I said, voice hoarse. "I'm sorry."

She kept her back turned to me. I'd betrayed her trust, and that came with consequences.

Two officers hoisted me to my feet. I couldn't meet their eyes. Dan was right, it had gone on long enough. I needed to face reality: I couldn't save Mona, and now, I had to witness what I'd done to her.

"I won't resist. I think I may need some help," I told the officers, keeping my hands out in front of me in case I needed to be cuffed.

"You're goddamn right you need help," John said before Bre silenced him.

"That's enough, Dad. He's going and can't bother her anymore."

In all the years I'd known Bre, I'd never heard her voice so cold, so detached. Whatever part of me she held onto, believed in, was gone, at least in her eyes.

"Sir, you can put your hands down. We aren't going to cuff you," the officer on my right said, tapping my shoulder amiably. We were all friends as long as I cooperated.

I nodded and made my way to the patrol car, its blue lights pulsing like a strobe lamp in the morning fog.

———

THE LAST THING I remembered from that day was the smell of gasoline in the air as we pulled away, my head leaning against the cool glass of the rear window. It had all come full circle, the alpha and the omega. My doorway of opportunity opened and closed with that smell, and I'd left Mona's demise worse off than it had been initially. I deserved everything I had coming, and I hoped they threw away the key.

I was moved to a mental health facility outside of San Francisco. Mona's father petitioned the court, and with the testimony of Bre and Dan, I was deemed a danger to myself and others. I'd mutilated my dead wife's body after digging it up, painting it with her blood, and scarring it, or so they said, even though nobody could prove where I'd gotten so much of her blood nor how the body of a person that expired a month before the incident could retain such fresh wounds. Still, as I was all too familiar with, sometimes rationality wasn't required to draw a conclusion and render judgment.

The therapists told me I had a dissociative break from reality, which wasn't an uncommon response for people with trauma, though mine was excessive. They didn't overtly tell me that last part, but I could read between the lines. To the whole world, I'd created the doorway and the visions in my mind because I couldn't let her go; my grief wouldn't let me. After a few months, I started to wonder if they were right. I'd already proven I couldn't handle trauma; I'd become a damaged, detached boy after my mother died and resisted almost every call to rejoin the world for years afterward. Why would it be so hard to believe I'd made up all the connections to Mona in my head to cope?

Time passed, and amid the monotony, I questioned the point of living. When I was a boy, I contemplated suicide, but the harsh reality of having to take direct actions to end my life terrified me far more than actually having to remain in this world. So I did nothing, hoping to minimize myself to the point that I just wouldn't exist any longer, akin to the old saying about the bear shitting in the woods; if nobody saw me, was I even there?

Music happened, jazz specifically, and then Mona. My existence became desirable yet tenuous, a gentle ripple able to push me off course, but I decided I wanted to be seen in the world, and I was. I lived, truly and deeply, with Mona. When she died, I struggled to find a reason to continue, that is, until I'd found her again. The music, like before, fueled my fire, but it was unsustainable without her. White shoes, white gowns, and white padded walls seemed the right environment for me to drift away into irrelevance. It's funny, though, that desire to live. Sometimes, when everything is at its most dire, that is when the epiphany comes. I finally remembered fully...

"IT'S SO HUMBLING BEING OUT HERE, isn't it? Away from the city and just listening to the woods. It's spiritual."

The stars were just beginning to shine through the blue sky as it transitioned to twilight. I turned my head from our open-topped tent to look at her profile, the scent of her shampoo wafting into my nose, filling me with the comfort of home in the gentle breeze.

"It's awfully quiet, that's for sure."

"Ugh, Trev, come on. There is so much around us if you just open up your mind. Listen to the wind; you can hear the whispers."

"Whispers?"

"Of those that came before us."

I shivered from a sudden caress of cold. It was like another presence crossed my path.

"There's something."

She grabbed my hand and gave it a squeeze.

Our eyes met.

"Please don't ever leave me," I said.

Her eyes became glassy, an accumulation of tears beginning to form.

"There will be a time when I'm not here anymore, Trevor, and you need to do something for me."

A pang of fear dug into my innards. My stomach hurt.

"Please don't ever say that."

"Sweetie"—she rubbed my cheek—"it will happen, so please listen."

Her eyes, there was something, the way her brows scrunched, that very same look from our rehearsal dinner so many years before. There wasn't doubt; I knew that now, it was determination.

"I need you to live," she said.

"What do you mean? What else would I do?"

She kissed me, something soft and warm, like feeling the first rays of the sun on a crisp morning. It was the feeling of life.

"Promise me."

"You are being ridiculous—" I protested, but she cut me off.

"Trevor."

"I promise, but can we stop now?"

Her lip quirked up in a grin, and she wiped away her unshed tears.

"Fly me away," she started our song.

"From this cold, dark place," we sang together, the sun's last light extinguishing behind the western horizon.

SHE WANTED ME TO LIVE, something that must come from within and not from others, and after all of my years, I understand. Alone, in a prison of my own making, I've finally found the will to carry on. I will live.

Sitting alone in my room, determined to see the sunrise from our tent in the woods again one day, I've found our melody again.

"Fly me away. From this cold, dark place. A bright escape. It's time to change my fate, today..."

PART TWO
NIGHT

DAS LETZTE WORT;
OR, THE FINAL WORD

"Was zum Teufel glauben die, wer sie sind?"

That fateful day was corrupted from the beginning. The windowpanes rattled as I stormed into my office, feeling low after the university board's harsh criticism of my current manuscript. Was I not one of the premier literary critics in Berlin? Did they think they knew better than me?

"Ficken Bastarde."

I tossed my briefcase onto my desk without a second glance and began to pace, roiling with contempt at the nerve of those usually spineless worms. I'd had enough. How dare they question me? Who did they think they were?

A sheaf of papers floated across my path. Startled, I shifted toward my desk just as the last vestiges of my manuscript scattered from their perch next to my typewriter.

"Nun, verdammt."

It just wasn't my day. I sat in my swivel chair, landing with a loud creak. Sighing, I leaned back and felt at ease. This chair was my seat of power, and from it I had destroyed the careers of many bright-eyed authors who thought they could be the next big success, all of them pushing their drivel as something of value. How satisfying it had been...

Why couldn't anyone write anymore? What happened to the days when masterful works following the likes of Faust and Siddhartha were created? Even some of those marginal English creations by Dickens were better than the cow dung that made it to my desk. What had happened to the brilliant prose of the classics? What were the great universities teaching these days?

I would have to ensure proper literature entered the public spectrum. God knows the masses didn't know what was good for them.

I leaned forward to retrieve the scattered pages, but I got tired quickly, resigning to fix them later. I couldn't contain my anger enough to concentrate on something so menial.

The gall!

I took a deep breath, released it, put a clean sheet of paper into my typewriter, and began to type. A little writing would be therapeutic, and the click-clack of the keys would be like a fine Bach symphony to my ears. I didn't plan on changing anything I'd written; the board could kiss my sizable arsch if they thought that would happen.

My *Leitfaden der Kritikin* would have been the greatest criticism text in the country, and students would demand its use in all of their literary graduate seminars. The University of Berlin couldn't tell the difference between manure and a diamond unless a master jeweler showed them, and guess what—I'm their master jeweler. If the university board needed reminding of that, so be it. They need to know that my opinion is the only one that matters, and my stamp of approval is the difference between success and failure. I will always have the final word.

Feeling more confident and self-satisfied, I reached into my right-hand drawer and pulled out my flask of Bärenjäger and a feather quill for corrections. Removing the stopper from the jar of ink, I started jotting down notes I wanted to incorporate into my text. This knowledge had to be shared. The future of literature depended on it.

After several minutes, my secretary walked in, as I knew she would, carrying a hot cup of tea. She was a despicable, unfortunate-looking creature that my loving succubus of a wife forced me to hire. She didn't want me to be attracted to the woman, and, needless to say, she was successful in her choice. Heaven forbid I had something nice to look at while I was working.

She approached my desk slowly, her double chin waddling as much as her saggy breasts and large midsection. She wore a polka-dot dress and a gaudy rose-shaped charm around her neck that appeared more like a choker than a dangling necklace. It was dreadful. To top it off, her hair was comically styled into a large poof atop her head, reminding me of a circus entertainer. I sighed as she approached.

"Hier ist Ihr Tee, Herr Schöble," she said, setting the cup down.

I leaned forward and smelled it. As usual, it reeked of fish. I don't know if it was the water she used or if it was her. She never looked clean per se, so I wouldn't be surprised, but the only time I was ever close to her was in those moments.

"Welche Art ist es?" I asked, unable to recognize the brew.

"Englisch Frühstück," she said, flashing her pointy yellow teeth in an attempt at a smile.

"Danke, das ist alles."

She turned about-face like a soldier and waddled back out of the room, the rolls on her back shifting up and down under her tight dress. The image of her ghastly face stayed in my mind a moment longer, and I shuddered and shifted my gaze back to my desk.

My flask shone in the dim light, and the Bärenjäger inside seemed to promise vitality like the Ambrosia of the old mythic gods. I succumbed to its summons, emptied it, nearly doubling the contents of my cup, and took a large gulp. My muscles relaxed, and I felt the day's tension drift away.

As if a dark cloud lifted, I finally had the clarity to get into my workflow.

The hour hand of my clock seemed to keep pace with the minute hand as time elapsed without notice, my fingers dancing along the keys like Beethoven during the height of a concerto. My strokes were masterful. I was in my domain.

Finally, I paused to stretch my fingers, curling them into a fist before expanding them outward. The room was black like a starless night in the country, save for the small aura of light emanating from my oil lamp. I didn't remember lighting it.

I looked around, my vision blurring when I moved my head too quickly. Had I drunk too much?

The room began to spin, slowly at first before gaining speed. Each rotation brought a new feature of the room to my attention. To start, it was the branches popping out from the bookshelves lining the walls, the room's constant revolutions causing them to rustle against each other and disperse leaves in the air. Then, the great bearskin rug in front of my desk melted into a pond with lily pads floating along its tranquil surface. Lastly, the twinkling glow of Blitzwanzen flickered here and there, which was the hallmark of my childhood exploring the damp forests in Bavaria.

I leaned back in my chair, awestruck at the sight and dizzy to boot. *I must be dreaming*, I thought, baffled by surroundings that could only be described as something out of Lewis Carroll's imagination.

Smacking my face, I tried to wake up from the bizarre dream, and with a sudden halt, the room stilled.

"You shouldn't hit yourself, old chap. That could leave quite a mark, eh?" an English voice said beside my left ear.

I flinched and turned my head to see a cock sitting on my shoulder, its comb and wattle a bright red against its otherwise white-feathered body.

"Vhere die hell did you come from?" I asked, realizing I, too, was speaking English, granted in thickly accented German.

"Don't mind him, kraut; the laddie tends to be full of shite anyway," said a feminine Irish voice to my right.

I froze, not wanting to see what this other creature could possibly be, as I felt its claws digging into my shoulder.

Vhat the hell? I thought, and looked to my right with a shrug. What difference did it make? I was stuck in this dreamland for the time being, so I figured I might as well find out. A fluttering of feathers buffeted my ears as I met the gaze of a small, brown hawk, its beady black eyes mere inches from my face.

"What's wrong, kraut? Does a puss have yer bleedin tongue?"

"Is zher a cat here too?" I asked, eyes wide.

"Heavens no, my good man. It is just the two of us. We are your advocates. That frisky Irish clover over there is your devil, and I'm your angel. It seems you've been a bit harsh with people lately, so we thought we should pay you a visit."

"Speak for yerself, English; I'm quite pleased with the bloody kraut. Keep tearin' the people down, ye Hun."

I stared straight ahead, avoiding looking at either of them. I was completely flummoxed. It was the strangest thing I'd ever experienced, whether a dream or reality. How odd, considering I thought I had a very vivid imagination.

"I don't know vhat the hell the two of you vant vit me, but I treat people just fine. Good day to both of you."

"Kiss my arse, kraut. Ye can't bloody push us off so easily," the hawk retorted.

I faced her, enraged.

"Listen here, paddy. I haf had enough of your name-calling! Do you know who you are talking to?"

I puffed out my chest, mustering all of my authority. This avian hoodlum wouldn't verbally accost me.

"To meself, you eejit! I am a part of ye, if ye hadn't realized it yet."

Why the hell is my bad side Irish and my good side English? I wondered. *Shouldn't my conscience be German?*

"What have we here? What a curious creature," interrupted the cock.

I scanned the room, losing patience with this insanity but interested in knowing what could be a more bizarre creature than the ones in this pair, and caught a blur of motion straight ahead. Beyond the still pond was the mouth of a cave where the door to my office used to reside. Standing there was indeed a most curious creature: a mighty winged fish, spotted white, with thorns and roses splayed out around its feet. It flopped several times on its rear fin, moving closer to me in a vaguely familiar waddle, a strong smell of fish wafting outward to fill my nostrils.

"Hellooo," the fish called in a musical yet obnoxious voice.

"Vhat the hell are you?" I asked, standing to confront the oddity. Reflecting on the situation, it was peculiar that I wasn't more apprehensive of the winged fish, but it seemed I had reached a point where enough was enough.

"What dooo yooouu meeean, Heeerr Schöble?" it asked in long, drawn-out notes that were distinctly off-key.

"Oh blimey, stick a knife in its arse, kraut! Shut its gob," the hawk instigated.

"Is that always your solution to everything? You are so bloody uncivilized," said the cock.

"Feck off, English"

"Vill all of you shut up?" I asked, trying to drown out their voices and the pseudo-melodious coos from the winged fish.

They both stopped, but the creature continued. It was the antithesis of the siren's call, its musical notes pushing me to the brink of violence. It stopped before me, its mere presence defiling the beautiful forest scene.

"Get out of my office."

The creature laughed, its gills opening and closing on its bulbous neck, releasing a noise like a clarinet with a broken reed.

"Oh, stop letting on, kraut; I know ye want to stab it. Ye have a knife in yer pocket," screeched the hawk.

Curious, I reached into my pocket and grasped what felt like the hilt of a knife. A small part of me was surprised to find it there.

"I'll be damned," I whispered as I pulled out the small pocket knife.

"No, old chap, don't do it! Don't let the devious leprechaun trick you," implored the cock.

"Shut it, English! Don't listen to him, kraut. Ye know ye want to do it. Shut that smelly thing up, eh?"

"You devil, do not corrupt the poor fellow. Listen, my good man, be a good sport and just ask it to leave."

"I'll claw ye to pieces, English, if ye don't shut yer gob! Do it, kraut! Shank it!"

The fish spread its wings and puckered up its scaly mouth, singing in a sharp whisper, "Dooo yoooouu waaant toooo stiiick meee, Heerrrr Schöble?"

I am not sure what came over me. It may have been the endless pestering of the two advocates, or maybe it was the cooing of that damn tone-deaf creature. Perhaps I am inherently a bad guy. Let's look at the situation seriously: I do love to torment fresh literary meat and rub their noses in the filth they call literature, so maybe it was just an instinctual response; a deep-seated hunger for aggression. In any case, something inside me snapped, and the Irish hawk won the argument: I decided to shank the thing.

The foul creature met my gaze, narrowing its eyes and thrusting its rotund body at me in some sort of perverse mating dance.

It was time.

With as much ferocity as I could muster, I thrust forward with the knife, leading from my hip in an attempt to conceal the weapon from view, and stabbed the fish over and over again. The sensation was exhilarating. All the aggression from the day's events melted away: the board of directors, the thought of my controlling wife, and the sight of that odious secretary. It's as if the murder of this creature was purifying my body in a fantastical baptism of violence. So, with a final orgasmic thrust, the creature fell backward into the pond, blood polluting its once-serene waters.

I felt like one thousand Goldmarks, and I leaned back to rest on the desk, letting out a satisfied sigh.

"Ye stuck it good, kraut; well done," praised the hawk.

"How could you be happy at a time like this? Good day to both of you. I can see I am not needed. Master Schöble," said the cock, spinning in on itself and vanishing in a puff of feathers.

"That damn English bird can never have any fun. I was only

slaggin 'im. Oh well, ye did good, kraut, ye pucked that thing real good. So long, ye fat arse."

In a similar fashion as the cock, the hawk vanished from my shoulder.

Finally, some peace and quiet; I savored the moment.

THE NEXT THING I recall is a loud crack startling me, and I sat up as one of the legs of my desk gave way. I was still on top of it, my head aching as though I had drunk four bottles of wine.

"Scheiße," I groaned, looking around the room. The light of midday was shining into my office. It was clear I had slept the night and the entire morning on my desk, and I could feel my back and neck throbbing.

Touching my feet to the ground, I stood up; a soft thumping noise echoed in my ears as if through a bullhorn. I looked down, startled by the auditory assault, to see my schwanz dangling out in the open for any onlooker to see. Adding to my horror, it was covered in dried blood.

Now let me tell you, nothing is scarier as a man than to wake up half-naked and have your favorite appendage looking this way. So, as you can imagine, I inspected it for injury, all the while distracted by the nauseating scent of fish in the air.

After being satisfied that it couldn't be my own blood, I remembered the strange dream I'd had the night before—a dream in which I killed something—a winged fish that smelled dreadfully like what it looked like. My eyes widened with that final turn of the mental key, clicking everything into place.

The haze of my memories cleared, and then the true course of events flooded my mind. I'd fucked my secretary. That corpulent, annoying, fish-crotched secretary. How did that happen? Had I been so drunk that I couldn't control my actions, and I had to picture myself in a fantastical place to justify an office affair? Considering the person, who could blame me?

Before my wife started mingling in my office, all the secretaries I had affairs with were gorgeous, which is probably why I did it. A man of my station needs someone on demand to relieve stress, and to be honest, my demon wife is a stress producer, not a stress reliever. Even so, how did I allow myself to fornicate with my beastly secretary?

I pulled up my pants, intent on running to the bathroom, when I tripped and fell to the floor with a loud crash. Then the door flew open and in waddled my secretary, a giant grin plastered across her face. Her eyes took me in like a cat about to dine on an unsuspecting mouse.

"Herr Schöble, was kann ich tun, um Ihnen zu helfen?" she asked, kneeling down in front of me and positioning her foul crotch within a foot of my face, the smell unbearable.

I will tell you what you can do to help me: go die, I thought, knowing that I wouldn't say it aloud in my current condition.

"Vhat happened last nacht?" I asked in broken English.

"Oh, you want to use English? Wonderful! I always love to practice. I studied it at university and lived in Britain for ten years, but you know that already. We talked about it last night. Is this our thing now, my darling? I knew I would win you over if only you gave me a chance."

I glared at her, hating her even more with each babbling word. I grabbed her hand and met her gaze, repeating my question more forcefully.

"Vhat happened last nacht?"

"Well, I knew you would be stressed from your meeting with the board, so I slipped some opium in your tea. When I came to check on you, you were quite out of it. That's not how the opium usually affects you, so I supposed you'd decided to pour in your whole flask of liqueur you always brandish about. But then, the most wonderful thing happened: you talked to me, I mean, really talked to me," she said, leaning back from me and brushing her hand across her forehead like a damsel in distress on the brink of fainting, fluttering her eyelashes at me. It made her look like she was having a seizure.

She continued.

"Most often, you ignore me, but not this time. I showed you I'd do anything for you, Herr Schöble. The opium I source for your stress, handling your wife, and not to mention my stenography skills. You see how invaluable I am."

A cautious rage started to simmer inside of me. The opium? My wife?

"Vhat do you mean?" I asked, straining to keep my face expressionless.

Her face brightened with deranged cheeriness.

"I told your wife about the other secretaries, of course. I've admired you from afar for so long, and I knew if I told your wife about your other affairs, she would intervene. I did it for us, darling. I had to get this job somehow, and aren't you glad I did?"

I sat up, feeling my shoulders tense as her scrunched eyes followed my gaze, our eyes locked. I didn't trust her being out of my sight for even a moment.

"Are you stressed, Herr Schöble? I'll get you some tea with a spot of opium. It keeps the edge off," she said, winking at me.

"How often do you put that in my tea?" I asked, the anger near boiling.

She waved her hand at me playfully.

"All the time! You are always so stressed. A powerful and famous man like you can't afford distractions like that. I can calm you whenever you'd like. You took my maidenhead last night, but I know I can give you the pleasure of a virgin still. I'm yours, you big, strapping, wonderful man."

A look of desire stirred in her eyes, accompanied by something similar to devotion, the type of look you see in a dog's eyes when it sees its master. Frankly, it made me nauseous, that and the thought of her blood all over my genitals.

What she'd said eliminated any of my doubts, though. I hadn't dreamt, nor had I lost touch with reality; I had been drugged. That crazy cow had tricked me and manipulated her way into my life. She plotted what happened, mapping out each point like a great novelist, and pounced when an opportunity presented itself. Sure, I'd fornicated with her while fully conscious, but who would believe it was uncoerced in my mind-altered state—I thought I was stabbing her, for God's sake!

I'd deflowered this sad, middle-aged woman, and she actually thought that by doing so, I would want to continue seeing her. Outrageous! Perhaps I should thank her, though. My drug-induced haze taught me something: I did truly want to kill her. Even before I'd learned what she'd done to me, I'd dreamt of ending her. I thought about what the cock in my hallucination had told me: don't let her trick me, and while the cock was referencing the hawk's temptations to violence, the sentiment still applied. I wouldn't be fooled.

That made it final. I am Wolfgang Schöble, the greatest literary critic of my generation, and what I think means everything. She wouldn't have the last word on this. I would.

"Vill you help me up?" I asked, sure to sound kind, although the bulging vein in my forehead would have been a telltale sign for all but the most intellectually lacking, which she certainly was.

She leaped up to obey, her mass shifting almost hypnotically as she helped me to my feet.

"To my desk," I said weakly.

As I turned around as if to sit in my desk chair, I decided it was now or never. In a swift motion, I grabbed my quill from my desk and stabbed her in the esophagus, pushing it through until it lodged in bone. Her eyes went wide as she pawed at her throat, loud wheezing piercing the silence as blood bubbled from the wound.

She collapsed, convulsing and flailing for several minutes before taking that satisfying final breath. I stood over her, smirking and feeling immense triumph over that old trickster as I'd had the last laugh.

It wasn't long before my first appointment came in and saw the mess on my office floor while I was leaning back in my chair, unconcerned, typing on my typewriter.

Shortly thereafter, the Polizei arrived to arrest me for my supposed crime, which is a shame because, to be quite honest, I found what I did to be a service to society. I'll have to send out news articles and statements, ensuring everyone knows precisely why it had been necessary. I'm not concerned, though; my fellow faculty members, hell, even the public at large, would agree with me—they always do, no matter what prison time I was being threatened with.

Anyway, that's how it all transpired. It is a shame that it happened this way, but here we are. I'm not worried; she was a nobody, so I bet I'll be out before I know it.

I'll have the final word.

Das Ende

THE LEGEND OF
CHUCKY MUDD

A full moon on Halloween, what a perfect time for a horror story. Connor had anticipated retelling his father's version all day, as it was more detailed than any others. He knew he could use it to maximum effect. Horror stories always scared him half to death, and, to be honest, he knew that's why his father liked to tell them to him. But they were just that—stories, and Connor could embellish them even further, instilling the paranoia necessary to make this the ultimate evening of torment, especially when it was the old town legend.

It was something Connor and his friends had done the last few years at school: the boys getting together to see who could one-up each other and frighten the socks off the others. Brock had always won, but Connor knew it would be him this time. Tomorrow at school, the story of Brock's terror would circulate, and Connor would be declared the champion.

Connor's mother overheard him talking about it when his father completed another retelling that morning, wanting to ensure Connor had it just right for his plan.

"Connor, don't you go telling that story to those boys. I didn't raise you to be cruel like that," she said, hands on hips.

His mother was a loving woman, always smiling and doting on every child she came in contact with. In the vein of that nature, she abhorred teasing and anything that even resembled bullying. He assured her until he was practically blue in the face that it was all in fun; none of them did it to be malicious, but she wouldn't hear it.

"Two wrongs don't make a right. If Brock jumped off a bridge, would you follow him right off the planks?"

Connor didn't even bother debating her. That's how she was, always trying to spread Christ-like intentions the world over, and with him entering sixth grade, she'd only become more vocal.

"Honey, he's fine. What are you so fidgety about?" Connor's dad asked, wrapping his arms around his wife and resting his hand on her stomach.

She placed hers over his and interlocked their fingers.

"It's probably partially this little one in here," she said affectionately. She was showing and knew she couldn't keep it a secret any longer, having just broken the news to Connor a month prior. He'd always wanted a sibling, but something about it didn't sit right with him. Maybe after his twelve years of life, going it alone, he figured, what's the point, though he'd never voice that opinion to his parents. He couldn't stomach the hurt it would cause; she loved so much, and this was what she wanted.

His mother looked his father in the eyes and held his gaze. It lingered, and a strange tension seemed to form in the air, which made Connor feel as though he was intruding. It lasted only a moment more before his mother let out a laugh, covered her mouth, and faced Connor. It was like a spell had been broken. He had goose bumps.

"I'm just being silly. Pregnancy brain," she said, giving herself a little tap on the side of the head. "I love you and be safe."

Connor nodded, unsure of what had just transpired, but warily decided that it was time to make his exit and turned to leave.

"Not so fast. Come give your mother a kiss before you go," his dad said, and Connor did so dutifully.

He gave his parents a wave and a smile and bolted for the front door. His dad knew he couldn't shirk his responsibility to his friends' tradition. This would spook them like nothing else had before, or Dennis at the very least, but that was just the start. The old town legend had been heard many times, but not this version. What if they could go and see the spot where it supposedly happened? It would be epic.

After leaving his house, Connor picked up his pace, the campfire smoke from his friends just up ahead in the waning daylight. He could just imagine them huddled around it, unsuspecting of his plans for the night.

A cool wind tussled the leaves above him, cutting through his light sweater. He could feel it deep within, like the aftereffects of being dunked in cold water; it was under his skin. He shivered, the hairs on his arms lifting as if saluting him.

Connor had one of those eerie moments where he thought he should choose a different course, one not so creepy, but he shrugged it off. After all, a story is just a story. It can't hurt you.

He veered off the sidewalk into a gap in the bushes, narrowly avoiding a pack of Care Bears and She-Ra Princess of Power—clad trick-or-treaters; Brock and Dennis were sitting on either side of the fire, poking it with sticks.

"Boo," Connor said, springing out from his cover in the foliage bordering Brock's backyard.

Dennis let out a high-pitched squeal, falling backward in the process. Brock stood but had little reaction other than rolling his eyes, his parachute pants, inspired by MC Hammer's "Can't Touch This" music video, swishing noisily.

"So terrifying," Brock said, deadpan.

Connor shrugged as he sat down on the woodpile opposite him.

"Dennis seemed to think so."

"Well, that's not saying much," Brock said, eyeing Dennis as he adjusted himself into an upright position again, face crimson.

Dennis, skinny as a rail and always dressed like one of the boys from *The Goonies*, couldn't catch a break from Brock's jabs. Connor often wondered why Dennis still persisted in being a part of their trio, but he figured Dennis knew that it was better to be on the good side of a meathead like Brock rather than his bad side. Brock was a dick, but he defended his friends fiercely.

"What took you so long?" Dennis asked, his voice quivering.

"I had to help my mom and dad with a few things around the house."

Brock got comfortable on his log before waving his hand at Connor. "Yeah, alright, I don't care about that. You think this is your year to win the Halloween scare-a-thon, so out with it. Let's finally hear what you got for us that you think will make you the champion."

Connor smirked and cleared his throat.

"It was on a Halloween night like tonight," he said, picking up the branch on the ground next to him and stoking the fire, sending a flurry of sparks into the air. Connor wanted to take it slow, really build up the drama. This story was good on its own, but greatly improved with theatrics.

"Seriously, Connor? A ghost story?" Brock asked, his eyes narrowing in displeasure.

"This isn't a ghost story, Brock. It's true; my dad told me so, and if you guys aren't going to be lame and chicken out, I figured we could go see where this happened once it's a little darker."

"See what?" asked Dennis, his voice cracking.

Connor sighed. Dennis was the easiest boy in their class to scare, practically always skittish. He actually took the fun out of it sometimes.

"Well, if Brock will stop objecting, I will finish my story, and then you will all know what 'it' is."

Dennis looked at Brock, meeting his gaze. They both nodded their heads and returned their attention to Connor, granting him permission to continue.

"As I was saying, it was on a Halloween night like tonight that it happened: the murder on Nokomis."

"Nokomis? Our Nokomis? Like the street we live on?" asked Dennis.

Connor cringed. He wasn't sure if Dennis's voice could get any higher, but he sure hoped it couldn't.

"The exact one. It happened sixty years ago, but there are whispers that what occurred that year had happened before."

"Oh, come off it, Connor! I thought you were going to tell us something new. This is just that old Chucky Mudd legend. My parents have tried to scare me into behaving with that tale since I was four."

Dennis nodded in agreement. "You better behave, or Chucky Mudd will come get you. Children who don't listen get taken away in their sleep," he recited with a shiver.

"Calm down, both of you, and give me a minute. You haven't heard this version before," Connor said, hands raised to quell their protests.

Brock closed his mouth but made a show of cracking his knuckles.

Connor cleared his throat.

"As I was saying, it happened sixty years ago that a man named Chucky Mudd moved to the neighborhood and onto Nokomis Street. Everyone thought he was a bit weird, often not being seen during the day, wandering the streets and nearby woods at night, running from anyone who approached him like a rat fleeing to the shadows. He spooked people. Mothers wouldn't let their children go out at night, and even the fathers started traveling in groups. The neighborhood was on edge, and not long after, Chucky became the victim of vandalism.

"It started slowly. Pranks like eggs thrown on his porch or toilet paper tossed into his trees, to name a few."

Brock and Dennis both perked up, looks of mischief blooming on their faces as they remembered some of their extravagant TP-ing excursions.

Connor leaned in closer, hands on knees.

"The authorities assumed it to be local teenagers doing it, but in those days, protecting the odd was not a priority, and they ignored it, leading Chucky Mudd to take matters into his own hands.

"One night a group of boys approached the house, carrying multiple sacks filled with dog shit, intending on lighting them on fire and hiding while Chucky attempted to stomp them out. The plan backfired.

"He didn't answer the door, but was walking home from one of his nightly prowls... And he saw as the boys placed the sacks in front of his front door, tongues of flame dancing in the dark, crisp night. Nobody is exactly sure what transpired at that point, except that the four boys went missing, and a baseball cap covered in blood was found in the bushes at the edge of Chucky Mudd's property."

Connor paused to let his words sink in, the other boys' eyes locked on to him. He had his audience captivated.

"Th-Then what happened?" whispered Dennis.

"A public execution.

"When they didn't arrive home, one of the boys' fathers set out to look for them, and that is when the cap was discovered. The boy's father went into a rage. You see, nobody in the town trusted Chucky, nor did they want him there, and the fear that had been building of what Chucky might be doing in the night seemed to be confirmed for the boy's father. It was time for Chucky to go.

"The man called on all of the people in the neighborhood, going from house to house and whipping them up into a lynch mob. Not a single person came to the defense of Chucky, not even the sheriff, all in a state of bloodlust at the sight of the bloody baseball cap.

"The town's eldest, an old crone living alone in a house beside the woods, told them it wasn't the first time an outsider had moved to town and taken children away. She had been young on the last occurrence, but the townsfolk had dealt with it before, and they would deal with it again. It was their right.

"They all gathered at the father's house before setting out for Chucky's, bats, knives, and crowbars in hand, anything they could find to bludgeon him with. They pounded on his door, but nobody answered, so the majority headed to the woods, knowing that was where he stalked at night.

"What they found shocked all those present: bodies of boys and girls hung from the trees that surrounded a small clearing at the top of the hill near the old schoolhouse; bloody entrails spread out like a Thanksgiving Day feast glistened in the light of the full moon. Sitting in the center of the carnage was Chucky Mudd, blood dripping down his chin and a far-off look in his dark eyes as he sang:

"*'It might be fun, but don't be dumb. To mess with Chucky Mudd is to guarantee you're done. He can't be hurt, he can't be killed. If you try to seek him out, your fate is sealed.'*

"A roar went through the crowd as they pounced on Chucky Mudd, his maniacal laughter echoing through the woods. They beat him until his body was broken, his bones nothing more than jelly within a black-and-blue bag of flesh."

Connor paused, looking from one friend to the other. They were both captivated, Dennis's Adam's apple bobbing up and down like a buoy in the waves. Even Brock looked nervous as sweat glistened on his forehead in the firelight.

"It was 1930, so while police back then weren't like Magnum P.I., the townsfolk knew they needed to get rid of the body. So, they made a pact to bury the body and to all band together, never to tell if anyone ever came looking for him. Chucky's remains were dumped in a hole they dug right where they'd murdered him. It was Halloween night.

"Over the next few days, the townsfolk pitched in, carrying wheelbarrows of gravel to lay atop Chucky's grave until they were able to source asphalt. The old crone warned her neighbors of the superstitions of her youth—that the child abductor at that time had claimed to be possessed by an old spirit, and because they didn't seal the grave, the spirit was able to come back. Nobody questioned her, and they sealed the ground to ensure that their collective secret was buried forever."

"What happened to the bodies of the children that were hanging in the trees?" asked Dennis, his voice squeaking.

"Nobody knows. It is said they just vanished. All those present were so focused on bloodying Chucky Mudd that they never saw what happened to them. All anyone knew was that when they had first approached, there were probably a hundred bodies hanging from the trees surrounding the clearing, wearing clothes from various time periods. Some looked like Pilgrims, and others looked like they had just stepped off the *Titanic*, the boys wearing suits with trousers that extended to the knees while the girls had on knee-length dresses. The only thing all of the children had in common was the gaping holes they had in their middles, right where their organs should have been."

"Holy shit," whispered Brock. "Now, that's a story!"

Connor beamed with pride. Brock never admitted a story was good, being the reigning champ. The first part of Connor's plan was done, and he knew Brock would insist on the next step.

"Okay, this asphalt mound—where is it? Wait! Is it the mound at the Keeling Recreational Center? Is that the resting place of Chucky Mudd?" Brock asked.

"Yep," Connor said, nodding.

"Damn! Every time we stood on that thing, we were standing on the body of that psycho killer. I can't believe it!" Brock let out a whistle before standing up and stretching, giving his knuckles another crack.

"I have another question," said Dennis, always the inquisitive one.

"What's that?" Connor asked.

"Where did Chucky Mudd live exactly?"

"Um, well... that's the really messed-up part. He lived in my house."

A piece of wood in the fire crackled. Dennis yelped.

"Yeah, I'm not sure exactly how my dad knows all the details. He moved to town when he was a kid and my grandparents bought the house from an elderly man that was going into nursing care. I can only imagine what he might have found," Connor said.

The boys nodded in agreement, and the level of tension in the air seemed to escalate tenfold. Connor felt as though he could reach out and touch it.

"Have you ever found anything weird in your house?" Brock asked.

"Not that I know of. You guys have seen our house, though. It definitely needs work and looks old, but the only weird thing I've ever encountered is a door under the stairs in the basement that won't budge. My dad keeps boxes stacked in front of it. He said the house has settled too much and is pushing down on the door, so it won't open."

"I wonder what's under there," Dennis said, eyes wide.

"Probably some of ol' Chucky's victims," Brock said, eyeing Dennis with a mischievous grin.

"I don't know about all that, but my dad did tell me if you go to the mound on All Hallows' Eve, you can hear the whispers of Chucky Mudd singing his song on the wind blowing between the trees, and if you repeat it, they say his spirit will appear," Connor said.

"That's bull," said Brock, shaking his head. "I don't believe that for a second, but I propose we check it out anyway. It's not Halloween without some jump-scares. You in?" Brock asked, leveling his gaze on Dennis.

It was evident, even in the dim light, that Dennis was shivering. Connor felt a little bad for Dennis, since Brock was the intended target, but he needed to toughen up. Dennis knew the tradition.

Brock put his hand on Dennis's shoulder and repeated himself.

"You in?"

"Yeah—ahem, yes," Dennis said, barely audible.

"All right, it's agreed," said Brock.

Connor looked around and noticed the full moon overhead, the cool wind blowing through the bushes just behind him. He could hear the distant mutters and laughter of costumed children on the breeze, and something else. He felt the hairs rise on his arms again.

It's just the wind.

He looked at his friends, their faces masked by shadow.

"We better get going. It's full dark now," Connor said.

Brock and Dennis nodded in agreement.

THE BOYS QUICKENED THEIR PACE, jogging to ensure they didn't miss their opportunity.

The streetlights flickered as they turned the corner from Shawnee Road onto Nokomis. The wind started to pick up, and a cold gust greeted them, chilling their cheeks. All three boys visibly shivered.

"M-Maybe we should head home," Dennis said.

"We're almost there. Stop being a wuss," Brock said, knocking his shoulder into Dennis and making him stagger. "Once we reach the end of Nokomis, we'll cross Algonquin Street and see if we can make our way onto the Keeling Rec Center grounds."

"Just make sure to keep quiet as we approach my house. It's a lot darker now, with trick-or-treat ending and everyone turning off their porch lights, but I don't need my mom to hear us and call for me to come home. Now, come on, pick up the pace," Connor said. The best part was still to come; he'd been waiting all day for this. Connor needed his friends to cooperate a bit longer.

"W-What's the hurry? Maybe we should go get flashlights and let our parents know where we'll be."

"Oh my God, Dennis. I swear I'm going to pound you into the ground if you speak again," Brock said, brandishing his fist.

Connor rolled his eyes and moved himself between them.

"Leave him alone. He can't help it. It will be fine, Dennis; it'll all be over soon."

Dennis dry-washed his hands, eyes darting from side to side.

"That doesn't make it any better, Connor. Something doesn't feel right."

Brock sighed, his irritation exaggerated for emphasis.

"Jesus, will you come on," he said, mumbling and storming off down the sidewalk.

Connor stared at Dennis for a moment, expression blank, before turning away to catch up to Brock, who had just reached the stop sign at the corner of Nokomis and Algonquin.

"Guys? Wait!" Dennis yelled and ran after them.

The boys crossed the street and ran across the open green leading up to the Keeling Rec Center's front doors. Their destination was in the back of the building, and as they veered left to go around the building, they encountered the chain-link perimeter fence.

"Shit, I don't remember where the gate is," Brock said as he eyed the fence, looking for an opening.

"It's on the other side of the building, but it's locked at night, you know that. We have to go through the woods. The wooded side of the playground and soccer fields don't have fencing," said Connor.

"W-Wait," said Dennis, stammering. "The s-same woods Chucky would go in-into?"

Connor shrugged. "Have a better way in?"

All three boys shifted their gazes to their left at the mass of trees that came right up to the side of the Keeling Rec Center and the chain-link fence. A breeze blew through them, ruffling the branches and leaves, the sounds almost like that of whispers.

"I don't know about th-this. I really th-think we should head h-home."

"Dennis," hissed Brock, "shut your mouth, or I will leave you here, tied up for Chucky Mudd."

Dennis gasped, his face turning skeletal white in the glow of the moon.

"I won't let him do that," said Connor, then mouthed *knock it off* at Brock.

"Watch me," Brock said, balling his fists. It seemed to be the only way he knew how to respond to any situation.

Connor gave him the finger before turning back to Dennis and wrapping his arm around Dennis's shoulders, guiding him forward.

"Let's go. Facing your fear is like ripping off a Band-Aid. It may suck for a few seconds, but then it's over, and you feel better."

Connor nodded his head toward the tree line and began walking in that direction, Dennis in tow. "We need to make our way through the woods from here and hook a right when the ground starts sloping upward. That should bring us out of the tree cover on the other side of the building, right next to the asphalt mound."

"And then what?" asked Dennis.

"Maybe we sing his song three times like with Bloody Mary or something," said Connor.

Brock snickered. "Oh yeah, that's right, and then this psycho is going to burst out of the ground and disembowel us? Give me a break," said Brock, his expression shifting to that of boredom. Connor was losing the upper hand.

Connor glared at his friend. "I never said he was going to disembowel us, Brock. My dad claims the legend is you'll see his spirit. It's worth a try, unless you're too scared."

"What did you just say to me?" Brock asked, his voice threatening.

"I don't want to do this!" Dennis said, cutting in.

"That's it!" Brock swiveled and socked Dennis in the mouth, the force of the blow knocking him onto his back. It all happened so fast that Connor didn't even register it until Dennis was already on the ground, his lip split open.

"God dammit, Brock," Connor hissed, swinging his arms. "I told you to leave him be. Plus, you idiots are going to get us caught with all this noise. We aren't supposed to be here after dark."

Brock glared at Connor, eyebrow raised challengingly. Dennis pushed himself up onto his knees, and Connor helped him to his feet. A line of blood dripped from his lip, and his eyes glistened with tears.

"I-I'm okay," Dennis said, sniffling.

Brock waved his hand at them dismissively.

Another cold gust of wind whistled through the trees, rattling the branches like an orchestra made of maracas. They all turned around in unison.

"Did you hear that?" asked Dennis, his voice a few octaves higher.

Connor nodded, a cold sweat saturating his armpits. He could have sworn he heard whispers. *This is going a bit too well*, he thought as he started to get the willies.

"Shall we continue into the woods?" Connor asked, forcing a smile.

They exchanged glances, each of them searching for the first sign of flight from the others, but none of them moved.

Brock broke their stasis, taking the first step, looking back at them challengingly. Connor knew that look; if they didn't follow, there would be hell to pay.

"Lead on," Connor said as he took a step and then another, followed closely by Dennis, joining Brock in the darkness of the woods.

The air around them seemed heavier, thick with the tension of the horrific possibilities lurking in the shadows.

Dennis kept bumping into Connor, trying desperately to stay with his friend without physically clinging to him. Connor was annoyed, but he'd brought it upon himself by driving Dennis to the extreme. He'd just have to deal with it.

After walking several hundred feet, Brock stopped and faced the other two boys.

"Sing that song, Connor," Brock said. "You know, Chucky's song from the town legend. Let's see if that asshole shows up."

Connor looked to Dennis, who was shaking his head vigorously. He knew Dennis didn't want this, and his mom's words about how he shouldn't terrify his friends started to nag at him.

I'm so close to winning.

"Brock, maybe we—"

"You aren't pussing out just because Dennis is whining, Connor. Sing it."

Connor mouthed *sorry* to Dennis and began to sing.

"It might be fun, but don't be dumb, to mess with Chucky Mudd is to guarantee you're done. He can't be hurt, he can't be killed, if you try to seek him out, your fate is sealed."

Connor looked around, the night air still and silent. He met Brock's gaze and shrugged.

"Er, aren't you supposed to say it a few times?" Brock asked.

"I said maybe we do that. I don't actually know for sure," Connor said, shrugging.

"Well, try it!" said Brock.

Connor continued, singing the song two more times, wondering if three times was really the magic number.

Don't let it get to you. It's all planned out.

"Now what?" Brock asked, shifting his feet back and forth.

"I don't know. Let's wait a few minutes and then head home if nothing happens," Connor said as he looked around.

Any minute now.

Dennis let out an anguished moan.

An icy breeze blew through the trees, kicking up leaves that the last gust hardly stirred, causing them to float outward at them like a wave.

A pang of worry churned in Connor's stomach as the cold air seeped through his clothes and chilled his skin. A crack sounded behind them, and Connor pivoted to try to locate where it came from.

The darkness and the noises started to get under his skin, with the natural movements of the forest being *too* good.

Another branch snapped in the distance, and Brock called out, "Make a circle," his voice cracking.

Dennis and Connor moved into position without argument, aligning so that they could collectively see in every direction, as they started moving again up the incline to the clearing, where the moon's light was just barely visible, where Chucky Mudd's resting place lay.

Another gust, more forceful than the last, howled through the trees after only a few steps. The air stung like that in the heart of winter, the cold biting their cheeks, leaving them feeling raw.

The howling subsided, and a gravelly whisper surrounded them, echoing as if they were in a chamber rather than the open woods.

"Run, run! Chucky's coming for fun. You sang his song, thinking he was gone. You thought you'd be safe; you thought it was just pretend, but saying his name thrice, your death it portends. There is nowhere to go, there is nowhere to hide, for once you call for him, it's time for you to die..."

As the taunt ended, Dennis let out a scream, bolting in a frantic dash, not caring where he was going as long as it was away from that place.

The other boys called out, telling him to come back, but he didn't listen. Hysteria took hold, and Dennis ran blindly down the hill away from the moonlight, deeper into the darkness of the woods.

"Maybe he has the right idea," Connor said, his teeth chattering as the temperature dropped, their breath visible in the air. He wasn't sure how this all was happening; the voice was one thing, but making the temperature drop wasn't part of the plan. He had a horrible feeling that something wasn't right.

What if Dennis gets lost? This is overboard.

Connor faced Brock, who didn't even acknowledge him. Brock simply ran toward the clearing at the top of the hill, where Chucky's mound lay at the edge of the Keeling Recreational Center's playground. Connor had never seen him move so fast, and it left him entirely alone.

"Wait for me," Connor called after Brock, trying to keep up. The feeling of wrongness crept ever deeper into his bones as another gust of icy wind blew across his face, causing his eyes to water. It felt as though the tears froze instantaneously on his cheeks.

As they crested the hill and neared the clearing, the branches began to creak and snap, revealing beams of moonlight in greater frequency like searchlights along a prison wall. Something was weighing them down.

Connor felt an object hit the back of his head, and the unexpectedness—the fear—took his breath away. He looked around, trying to find the culprit, but nothing was in sight until he heard another snap and looked up, and with a gasp, fell onto his back.

No! Oh God, Dad! Where is he? This isn't right; none of this is right.

"Dad," he choked out as his chest tightened.

Connor wanted his parents then. His dad, yes, who was supposed to be there with him for this part of the plan, but he wanted his mom even more so. He thought of how she had worried over him and not wanted him to go scaring his friends. He wished he'd listened. He wished he could go to her then and give her another hug, safe in their house, but there was nothing for it. Connor had invited death.

Hanging above his head, and swinging in the wind from left to right, were the bodies of children roughly his age. Some were white, some were black, some were skinny, some were fat, some wore dresses, and some wore pants. All different, but all had one thing in common: gaping holes in their torsos, where their empty abdominal cavities streamed blood that glistened like lake water in the light of the full moon.

Brock fell to his knees a few feet in front of Connor and begged to be let go.

"Chucky, we were just messing. Let me go. P-Please, let me go." His voice was quavering as tears drenched his face.

Connor knew deep down that they'd awoken something that should have been left alone. This was all meant to be a prank, something he orchestrated with his dad's help to scare Brock once and for all—a story followed by a trip to the woods where his dad jumped out wearing a Leatherface mask; no more, no less. But this—this was real. How could this be happening? It was supposed to be just a story.

Snap.

Above Connor, a shadow descended, and he flattened his body against the ground, praying that if he just stayed still, he might not be seen.

Something wet hit his face, and he wiped it away, looking at his fingers.

Blood.

Eyes wide, Connor focused on the body above him as it turned to face him.

Dennis's eyes were lifeless—milky—with a gaping hole to match the other bodies, torn out of his midsection, his blood dripping out in rivulets.

Connor screamed, and Brock jumped to his feet, pushing Dennis's hanging body out of his way in his fight to make it clear of the tree line.

Brock entered the clearing, heading directly for the asphalt mound. The moon's glow bathed him in light, leaving Brock looking like a prisoner who'd been flashed by the watchtowers, exposed and hunted. His movements were erratic as fear took hold and fight or flight was the only thing his body could comprehend.

Brock's foot made contact with something slippery, and he lost his balance as his right leg kicked out at an unnatural angle with a crack.

Connor watched him fall face-first and slam his head against the mound.

"Ahhhh," Brock yelled, his knee bent in the opposite direction of what it should be.

Connor tried to get up and go to his friend, but it was as though his limbs were stuck in quicksand, unable to move. He could only lie there, frozen in terror, as a human-shaped silhouette of darkness approached Brock like the angel of death. There would be no escape.

The figure got closer, its movements slow and deliberate, its shadow swaying in a serpentine fashion. It was an apex predator toying with its prey; it had no reason to rush.

"Well, well, well. Looks like another one fell into Chucky's web," the gravelly voice said.

Brock opened his mouth to scream, whether it was for help or his life, Connor didn't know, as his throat opened in a razor-thin gash from one side to the other in a spray of blood.

Connor tried to scream for help, to save his friend, but no sound left his lips. It was as if every last defense mechanism he had, failed him. If only he could run, but where would he go?

The playground was in front of him, maybe twenty feet or so away from the asphalt mound, but it, too, was covered in blood. Organs, ranging from intestines to livers, dangled from the monkey bars and the swings; it was a sight out of his worst nightmares. No matter if he went forward or if he turned back, he wouldn't be safe.

The dark silhouette shifted and turned its gaze on Connor; its attention brought a piercing cold that penetrated his bones. He wanted so badly to run, but his legs felt like gelatin, hardly strong enough to even stand on.

"Connor, Connor, Connor," said a voice in a hiss. It was little more than a whisper, and he could feel its breath on his neck.

Another gust of wind blew through the trees, and the frosty air seemed to breathe life into the hanging bodies. Their mouths started to move.

"It might be fun, but don't be dumb, to mess with Chucky Mudd is to

guarantee you're done. He can't be hurt, he can't be killed, if you try to seek him out your fate is sealed."

Connor's bowels emptied as the raspy chorus came from the dead children, their bodies swaying in the wind. Even Brock's mouth began to move, spurts of blood squirting out with each motion of his jaws.

Connor lost all sense of reason or control, and his legs began to move, propelling him forward toward the playground without processing what was in front of him.

The shadow raised its arm to reveal a large rusty knife, and as though removing a veil, his features were exposed to the moonlight. Chucky's skin was pale and blotchy, and the folds of his neck did not quite connect.

Chucky held out his empty hand and stopped Connor before he could cover any ground. A smile spread across his face, lips split and chapped, with blood dripping down from the corners of his mouth.

"You did well, Connor."

Connor's face paled a ghostly sheen. He'd failed to make any ground; he was trapped. It was just him and Chucky. Nobody was going to save him.

"W-What did I do?" Connor asked, voice cracking and hardly louder than a murmur.

"You know what you did. You told them the tale I shared with you earlier, and then you brought them to me as we planned."

"B-But my dad told me—"

Connor broke off, eyes widening at the implications of what had just been said.

"No...," Connor said, eyes filled with tears. His legs began to wobble, and he nearly collapsed. "I-It can't be. This wasn't what was supposed to h-happen."

The man raised his hand to his face and dug his nails into his chin. A squishing sound, like that of ground meat when it is mashed between fingers, was heard as the facade was slowly pulled away. His father's face was beneath it.

Connor shook his head as if that could change the truth.

"D-Dad?" he asked, tears like small rafts of sorrow rolling down his cheeks.

"Let's not have any of that," his father said, drawing the edge of his knife across his son's cheek to flick a tear away.

Connor wanted to recoil, to run and scream, but he couldn't—not from this man, not from his father.

"D-Dad... my friends... why?" Connor asked. He couldn't wrap his head around how what was supposed to be a prank turned out to be nothing more than a ruse, a plan for his father to satisfy some kind of sick desire to kill. His dad was supposed to be his protector. He'd looked out for Connor and his friends, not kill them.

This can't be real. Something got him. Chucky got my dad!

"Are you Chucky Mudd?"

"I am now." His father lowered his knife and looked down at Connor. Connor could feel the warmth in his father's eyes, that love radiating outward that he'd always bestowed upon him, but he could also see the darkness, his eyes not reflecting any images or light from the moon.

"It is time, son."

His father reached out and rubbed Connor's hair. His dad would always do that to him when he was little, which Connor took to be affection. Now, it felt like nothing more than praising a pet, one that delivered his friends to be slaughtered.

"You see, Connor, the residents of our little town have always known of Chucky Mudd, or at least they knew they needed to feed the spirit; that's why they made the deal so long ago. This land didn't belong to people who look like you and me, but they took it anyway."

His father was staring off toward the woods, eyes unfocused.

"You've learned about what European settlers did to the Native Americans in school, but you won't find everything in a textbook. Things happened a bit differently here, near the southern Mississippi. There was a truce, you see. Something deeper, more spiritual, connected to this land.

"The Choctaw called it Impa Shilup, the soul-eater. They feared this creature of shadow so greatly that they wouldn't even utter its name. That is until desperation led one of their tribe to do so.

"As his people lost ground to the men with guns, the native summoned Impa Shilup, chanting his name and offering his soul, if only his people would be spared. The being obliged.

"The tide of the massacre swayed in the Choctaw's favor as the possessed native ravished the English settlers and militiamen. As the English casualties mounted, their thoughts turned dark and genocidal, becoming even more savage in their attacks on the Choctaw, shifting from just defeating their men in battle and occupying their land to murdering women and children en masse, whether it was marshaling them into structures to burn to the ground or flaying their bodies and making flags with it to taunt their warriors.

"Impa Shilup glorified the malevolence, drinking it all in like one who discovers water in the desert. Each new death made him more powerful and amplified his influence until his bloodthirstiness started to consume everyone and everything. The Choctaw were losing control of what they'd unleashed."

Connor was transfixed, fear holding him in place as his father recited this history.

"But why—"

"Don't interrupt me," his father said, voice sharp, as his eyes locked back onto Connor's.

"Now, as I was saying, the tribal leaders knew the creature drinking in their deaths and those of their enemy, but they feared its wrath if they interrupted its feast, so they concocted a plan—a bargain of sorts.

"They sent envoys to the English, who knew of the wild native they spoke of. Being God-fearing Anglicans, they agreed to talks to stop a demon. It was then that the great truce was made."

His father's eyes widened, his pupils becoming dark pools that consumed his irises, leaving behind only the faintest halo of white.

"The fighting stopped, drawing Impa Shilup out. The warriors of each side met the spirit here in the forest, at this mound," Connor's father said, waving his hand at the asphalt mound near Connor's feet, Brock's blood-covered body splayed over it.

"Impa Shilup raged at the peace, and they presented their offer. If the killing would stop, if Impa would curb its murderous miasma, the natives and the colonists would agree to peace and live on this land in perpetual coexistence. In return, they would ensure Impa Shilup would always have souls to feed upon.

"Impa laughed at this, saying bargains had no dominion over it. The two sides implored it, reminding it that if the fighting continued, they would all be dead, and there wouldn't be any souls left for it to consume; it would be left in a vacuum of starvation. While Impa was a being driven by its hunger, it wasn't foolish. It accepted the bargain and told the warriors to bury it and bring its sacrifices to its burial grounds, and in return, it would offer protection, a kind that would make this land a haven that wouldn't be found anywhere else. But Impa deceived them."

His father stepped away from Connor, knowing he was rooted to the spot and wouldn't dare move. Connor would never disobey his father.

Moving to the tree line, the shadows around his father grew deeper, like a cloak, blurring his features, except for his mouth. Connor could see his lips, pursed as if sipping from a straw, and wisps of air, colored in faint hues of red, white, gray, and green, were inhaled into him, making the shadows ever darker.

He became a void, except for his face.

His father turned back to him, his eyes now obsidian pools.

"You see, the peace only lasted a time, as Impa grew restless, playing off the English prejudice he knew they could never truly overcome. Their thoughts didn't stray enough for Impa to leave its grave and take over their bodies, but a cloud began to spread through the newly formed town. Mistrust and resentment festered, and then, some outsiders—a small family from the New England colonies— moved here into a cottage just over there."

His father's hand formed out of the mist to point in the direction of where they lived.

"The father of the outsider's family didn't like having to live side by side with the Choctaw. He thought they were savages and that the other English colonies in the Americas brought the natives to heel much more effectively. He shared his thoughts with the town's Englishmen, and while they agreed, they kept the nature of their bargain a secret, as outsiders weren't a part of the truce.

"Eventually, the father decided to take matters into his own hands when, at the village schoolhouse, a group of Choctaw children tried entering the school while he was still inside after escorting his children in. He took out his pistol and used the butt of it to pummel the Choctaw children, bloodying several of them before a handful of Choctaw men arrived to investigate the commotion. The father was beaten to within an inch of his life.

"The town's Englishmen knew the outsider brought it upon himself, but Impa's tendrils had already insidiously stoked the flames, their prejudices being too deeply ingrained to ignore, especially with the outsider recently speaking of them in the open. They whipped themselves into a furor at the savage Choctaw; why should they have to share anything with them, they'd asked themselves. That was when they wavered no longer. The English pounced.

"The killing began again in earnest between the Choctaw and the English, but this time, the English approached the mound and offered a new bargain. Impa would be free to walk among them, and they would help feed it if it freed them of the natives. Impa had no loyalties to simple humans.

"It agreed readily, creeping inside the battered and broken outsider, relishing in his thoughts of revenge. The man's name was Charles Mudd."

The shadows began floating toward Connor, wisps of darkness reaching out to tug at his shirt sleeves. Connor felt emptied: his bowels, his voice, and now, even his fear. What had frozen him in place before seemed to have thawed a bit, and he felt in possession of his legs once more. He took a step back and then another until his feet were grasped by the darkness.

"Connor, you wouldn't be trying to walk away from me, would you? I thought I taught you more respect than that."

Connor tried to protest, but his throat and mouth were too dry and raw to produce words. He would do anything his father said if he would just not hurt him.

"Anything?" his father asked.

Connor gasped.

He can hear my thoughts!

"Dad, please," Connor said, voice practically inaudible. It hurt him to speak as more of the shadows grasped onto him.

"It was supposed to be you, Connor. This was your test. My time as Chucky was supposed to end; I was finally meant to be free.

"Impa is ready for a fresh soul, but you disappoint us. You see, people would kill to live in this town with its village feel and excellent schools. Lord knows I have, and so did the man who became Chucky sixty years ago.

"Since I was a boy, I've fed Impa. I found the old Chucky's tools in our basement when my parents bought his house. I was drawn to them by a voice in my head beckoning me to the small door under the stairs in the basement. That's where I found this," he said, holding up the rusty knife and the mask made of skin. "These belonged to the last Chucky, the one from the story."

His father's obsidian eyes looked at the asphalt mound, and the cloud of shadows shifted as if nodding.

Connor shook his head as if trying to wake himself from a dream, but to no avail; he was living this nightmare.

"The first tribute of mine was a neighborhood friend. I didn't want to do it, but Impa demanded it, and soon, I lost the will to resist. I felt sick for days afterward as the newspapers reported the missing child, while police sent search parties throughout the town and the woods near the mound, but when no trace of my friend was found, I felt better, and a gnawing hunger began eating me from the inside. Impa wanted more.

"Have you ever wondered why you never met your grandparents? They didn't die of natural causes, as I led you to believe. They each took their turn under Chucky's knife: my father when I was a teenager and my mother when I was in my twenties before I met your mother. I told neighbors that they wanted to be buried where they met in Philadelphia, but they died here just like so many before them —as a meal for Impa Shilup.

"I think many of the elderly residents in the town suspected that something was amiss, as they'd been around for the killing of the Chucky Mudd in 1930, but they kept their silence, instead using the story as a tale to scare children into compliance. They probably thought it might even save some of them, but it didn't, for the easiest meat for Chucky to find were those who taunted him in his woods, and children just like you and your friends came willingly and frequently."

Connor's eyes drifted to the bodies of the children hanging in the trees over his father's shoulders. He could feel the panic rise inside him, but it was too late. He couldn't move his arms, his legs, and now even his head as the shadows cradled it like a newborn babe, forcing him to stare at all the children who had been taken before him.

He's a monster! Mom can't know about this.

"Oh, she knows. She's known about me for a long time. Living in that house does something to you, Connor; Impa has a hold over both of us, and we've accepted our place.

"It is time for a new Chucky. Impa grows tired of my body and my emotions; he craves something new as he always does in time. I had hoped you would come to understand and take your place in my stead, but I can see now that won't ever happen. You are much too soft. Such a pity."

Connor met his father's eyes and knew there would be no going home again. There was no shred of his father left in that gaze. He was Chucky Mudd through and through. This would be his final moments.

His father's arms breached the shadows like the hull of a ship splitting a wave, one hand holding the rusty blade and the other the skin mask.

"Goodbye," he said, the gravelly voice of something otherworldly coming from his father's lips.

Pulling the skin mask back on, Chucky Mudd and all the bodies of the children hanging in the trees began to chant:

"*Run, run! Chucky's coming for fun. You sang his song, thinking he was gone. You thought you'd be safe; you thought it was just pretend, but saying his name thrice, your death it portends—*"

Connor didn't have time to register anything else that happened. His mind raced through his memories with his parents, of them raising him, loving him, nursing a skinned knee, Little League, and movies on the couch; all the while, he wondered why they'd sacrifice so much of themselves for him, just to give him over to Impa Shilup like so many other children before him. It was as though they raised him like a calf, knowing they'd butcher him in the end.

Connor tried a final time to plead for his life, but no sound came out as the rusty knife in his dad's hand careened through the air and sliced his neck in two, silencing him forever.

CONNOR'S DAD walked into their house with a sigh as the day's first light started to peak over the horizon.

"Honey? I'm home."

"I'm in the kitchen. Do you need a beer?"

"God, yes," he said as he walked into the room, meticulously arranging his shoes and duffel bag on the floor near the door. He'd never let Connor get away with a mess. He would keep that example.

His wife glanced around the corner and met his gaze, her mouth a straight line betraying nothing.

He kept his eyes on her as he stepped into the kitchen, giving her a kiss on the lips and taking the beer from her hand.

"How'd everything go?" she asked, though the watery shimmer in her eyes revealed she already knew the answer.

"Not as we'd hoped. It feels quiet for now, at least," he said, taking a seat and tapping his finger against his head; the voices, the urges, satiated once more for a time.

She sat as well, taking a deep breath before making eye contact again.

"And Connor? Is he…"

"With the others," he said, watching her. He knew it would be difficult. They'd loved their boy, but there wasn't room for someone who questioned, for someone soft. She'd known that.

"It was the only way," Connor's mom said, nodding. She stood and walked over to the window, watching the light of the new day stretch over their back lawn.

There was nothing they would need to explain. Chucky never left a trace of the children he'd fed to Impa. They would grieve publicly, just like Brock's and Dennis's parents, garnering the sympathy of the town as search parties went out looking for the boys. Nothing would turn up, as usual, and the other boys' parents would leave town while Connor's mom and dad would be looked at with pity as another set of parents who had lost a child, their son's story being another one of those whispered about as being a victim of the town's legend: Chucky Mudd.

Connor's father stood and walked over to his mother, wondering if she had any regrets about what he was, about what had to be done.

"Dear, are you all right?" he asked, placing his hand on her stomach. He felt a kick from the baby within.

She turned her head to face him, her cheeks covered with tears, yet her eyes and smile exuded joy.

"Yes, we still have time." She let out a small hiccuping laugh and placed her hand over his on her belly. "And I have a feeling this will be the Chucky Mudd we need."

They kissed, tendrils of shadow linking their hearts to the baby in her womb. Within her, the baby opened its eyes and smiled.

SCALPEL

It started with a cut, or so they tell us, but who can be sure? A lot has happened since then. Pockets of life are now as sparse as water in the desert. We hide and make do, but we are no longer the hunters; humanity's dominance over the world has been exposed for the farce it always has been. Nature is the true lord of the Earth.

I'm lucky this group found me. Most of the compound mates I was housing with had perished, and our supplies had run dangerously low. These newcomers promised protection and food as long as we let them through the gates. I had little choice.

You see, my skills are useful only for my intellectual curiosity, as we lack the materials we had before the world divided. I'm a man of science, but what good is that now when we must cower in our hovels and pray that we don't draw notice?

I can't hunt or build a shelter. I'm a product of the pampered society we all hail from, unable to survive if civilization collapsed. I need protectors.

Communication has been scant. We tried to grow our community to become self-reliant but hardly ever made contact. We depended on old, beat-up CB radios and Morse code, but both became unreliable as the old infrastructure continued to rot. We've sent groups of brave men and women to repair the lines or supply a generator to failing stations, but we lost them just as quickly as we've lost everything else. A hasty demise seemed to be the only certainty any of us had left.

It's so hard to recall how it all happened.

I wish I had the internet to verify what I remember watching, but that is also a thing of the past. The Fall came so fast that as it played out, it was too difficult to discern a deepfake from reality. Disinformation had already become too embedded to trust what our eyes and government told us.

"It's a political stunt" and "fake news" were the catchphrases tossed around, carryovers from the last great pandemic. This time, though, we needed more than masks, and social distancing took on a new meaning.

The man looked up, hearing a cough through the paper-thin walls of his room, the lights flickering. Shadows dominated every nook and cranny of the small space, their hidden depths striking fear in his belly like an assassin's knife. He could see figures stirring in those shadows, phantoms of lives lost. Too many lives...

He shook his head and wiped his hand across his brow.

Bzzt.

The lights flickered again. This happened more frequently as the fuel for the generators became limited. He hoped today wasn't the day they permanently went dark.

The lights finally steadied, and he let out a relieved sigh. He set down his pen and walked to the window, dry-washing his hands to calm his nerves. This little corner of humanity still lived. There was still hope.

Leaning against the casement, the man rested his forehead on the cool glass of the window. The bright moon illuminated the compound's small courtyard and the security fence that traced its perimeter. He tried to remember how many days he'd been there—or should he think months?

The fence shook, a gentle sway that was enough to draw his attention. He held his breath as several hundred people shuffled around on the other side, their outlines faint. There was no rush of movement, just a little rattle—a testing.

He exhaled, relief washing over him.

The compound was still safe.

He returned to the table, trying to center himself as he walked, and then sat down, nodding.

He picked up his pen.

It started with a scalpel, to be more precise. Improvements in the healthcare system and sterilization methods of our medical units created a false sense of security.

They were necessary after 2020. Years of better air filters and safety precautions, put in place with massive funding by the federal government to protect us against our airborne enemies, should have eradicated any threat.

Hospitals around the country stocked up on N-95 respirators, and even the smallest clinics were built with negative-pressure rooms. We felt we were infallible, but we were fools. The next respiratory virus wouldn't catch us with our pants down, not again. But what of the ones that came by way of touch?

The earliest reports came from the Midwest, and China quickly jumped on the chance to excoriate our nation for it, much like we did to them with the outbreak from Wuhan, a tit-for-tat. Who could blame them?

It was insidious, this germ. Even now, I don't know what to call it. A disease, I suppose. The rapidity with which it activated and moved through the population was unheard of. It was like it had been biding its time, a sleeping giant waiting to wreak its havoc. The thing is, I'm not even sure if we discovered when it took hold before the Fall, but we had definitely seen what it was like.

In the late 2000s, like millions of people before her, my grandmother lost touch with reality after her Alzheimer's diagnosis, and my family had to cope with it. She didn't know any of us as she reached the end.

Alzheimer's has been called the silent epidemic, and the medical research had been on to something in naming the phenomenon. What I witnessed in my grandmother's decline was a taste of what was to come.

You see, the germ did the same thing, wiping out memory and recognition, but it was more than that, which is why it was so perplexing to diagnose. At first it was impossible to tell who had dementia and who didn't. Which patients were really a kind of sleeper cell teetering on the brink of wreaking devastation rather than just fading away?

It's confusing, isn't it? It's almost as though I am saying that cognitive diseases mutated into something even more sinister, and that is partially true, but it had more to do with the root causes.

The germ broke out in nursing homes, exploding into the patient population as many novel illnesses do—or at least that was the initial shot that started the war, one might say. Once that first visual of bizarre behavior was recorded at a small eldercare facility outside of Chicago, hysteria ensued, with cities issuing shelter-in-place mandates as the germ's blitzkrieg advanced deeper into the general populace. It was a 9/11 moment in the media.

Death wasn't the result, we all heard on the news—or it was, but only cognitively. The bodies remained quite active and aggressive. CCTV images of the elderly dragging themselves across floors to rip the flesh from a nurse's heel and that news report of a grandmother biting the face of her four-year-old grandchild and ripping her cheek off were the alarm bells. Nursing facilities went into immediate quarantine nationwide.

You see, it spread through saliva and bites as the infected attacked the healthy. It sounds a bit like rabies, doesn't it? That was one of the first theories—thinking it had evolved into this new, more insidious variant—but the thing is, this germ wasn't even a virus.

For decades, movies and comics portrayed zombie tales with origin stories that described mutated viruses, creating corpses to roam the Earth endlessly, looking for brains. I'm not saying this germ created zombies, but the aggressive, brain-dead actions of the infected seemed terrifyingly similar.

Humans became feral, starting with the mental decay of the eldest among us.

Amyloids—the vicious little proteins that accumulate in the human brain—changed somehow; they were the true culprit, no longer just creating stationary cognitive barriers but spreading, moving through a host like the viruses they had been mistaken for. They already caused Creutzfeldt-Jakob and Alzheimer's diseases—the amyloids building up and destroying the mind—but spreading like this? Through the touch of protein-laden fluids? It was like some kind of next step in a biological assault on humanity.

He shivered and blew on his hands. The heat became even more of a luxury when the fuel necessary to keep the lights on became so rare. He pulled out a pair of raggedy crocheted gloves that were tucked behind the pouch fastened to his belt, snags of yarn sticking out in various spots, and pulled them on.

The lights blinked off again.

He stood up, bumping the table with his leg and spilling ink on his notebook.

Just breathe, he told himself as he slipped toward hyperventilation. It would be okay, he was still safe.

He felt around in the dark, hands reaching in the faint moonlight to find the cabinet near the sink. He kept his flask of moonshine there, the drink sometimes the only safe source of hydration since the water pipes had run dry and the availability of untainted drinking water became a rarity.

They'd reverted to medieval practices, boiling whatever muddy water they could find and relying on crude distillation processes to make it as sanitary as possible, but also, their reality was hard and the need to numb it was ever-present. So, in that moment, the moonshine played its dual role as intended—a nip to calm his nerves.

The lights turned back on, and he sighed, taking an extra swig.

The chain-link fence rattled again, and his heart began to beat faster. A feeling of lightness hit him, the body's response to his mind telling him to flee.

"They're getting agitated," he murmured.

The clanging lasted a few more seconds and then quieted. The night was still once more.

Removing the gloves, his palms now sweaty, he sat back down at the table and retrieved his pen.

It started with contamination, that unclean scalpel used in an emergency operation. I know I said it was a cut, and this is the one I'd referenced: the slice of cranial flesh. An

Alzheimer's patient in Chicago had fallen and hit her head, leading to a brain bleed that required immediate surgery.

Surgeons involved with the operation swore under oath that they'd used the autoclave to sanitize all the utilized equipment, but what does their testimony even matter after what happened? They are long since dead, and they didn't know the proteins couldn't be removed.

According to reports and security footage, amid surgery on the parietal lobe, the patient opened her eyes and lunged into an attack. Head open and bleeding, she had to be shot and killed by a security guard before she was stopped, but it was too late. Pandora's box was opened the moment that knife touched her flesh and unleashed the mutated proteins into her bloodstream.

British journals had already been talking about the stickiness of amyloids since the mid-twenty-teens. Those protein aggregates clung to whatever they touched and adhered like overly wet bread dough, defiant to sterilization and spreading from person to person as hospital equipment was used. Humanity's greatest nightmare had become realized: proteins had become contagious.

But how did they cause accelerated brain degradation like something out of a horror movie? I have been struggling to find out. We all have since the beginning. But humankind is losing. There are so few communities left that any knowledge we have is likely lost, my past colleagues nothing more than a memory.

I studied medicine before the Fall. It felt like a different age then, filled with bright lights, skyscrapers, and instant access to information. It's amazing how deceptive time can be with trauma manipulating my perception of months to seem as though they were years. What I wouldn't give to have my *life before all of this back or, at the very least, the knowledge to do something about it. I never thought I'd miss that iPhone that my son was always trying to steal for himself, but now I'd give anything to trade for it.*

Early on, this compound was a fortified refugee camp. We had armed protectors, but that only lasted a short time. As food dwindled, so did our protection.

Battling hunger, I've forgotten much, each day feeling more protracted than the one before it. I often wonder how I am still alive.

In the dystopian novels I used to consume like water before the Fall, when leisure time was safe to enjoy, there was always a big event that took down everything. But the authors rarely explored the smaller particulars: vulnerabilities of humanity that could shed human lives like a dog sheds hair when our safeguards collapse. That's what claimed most of those inside our compound walls. Nothing big or catastrophic. Just a slow degradation.

Sure, several of my compound mates got caught by the infected while out scavenging for food, eviscerated like a young deer by a pack of wolves. Still, outright starvation and disease from dirty water became the more significant threat. It's hard to know how much time we have left.

A snap, like that of a broken cable, a metallic poiiing, followed by the clanking of the chain-link fence, broke the silence in the room. The man felt his heart flutter.

"Shit," a voice called out from the outer courtyard two floors below, a barrage of gunshots following closely behind.

He looked down to his notebook at the last sentence he'd written.

It's hard to know how much time we have left.

"I've condemned us."

A guttural roar rattled the room's window and was followed by raspy inhalations that sounded like snarling dogs.

The gunshots ceased.

Screams erupted in the hallway outside of his room. A flurry of activity shook the floor. His compound mates were in a panic, driven by their need for survival. Urine ran down his leg as he looked toward the window, the bestial sounds increasing in volume.

He ran over to the window, his mouth opened in horror of its own accord. The fencing had been torn open, and bodies of the infected pooled in like water from a burst dam. There would be no stopping this tide.

Wahoooom.

Bass with no treble rippled through the room as the power generators shut down, plunging the man into darkness.

He followed the disparate noise with his own. "Everything has failed."

Glass shattered somewhere on his level in the building, followed by the stomping of feet and panicked screams... they were coming. He began to shiver, his breaths becoming shallow as he tried to control his rising hysteria and take in enough oxygen through the smell of the burning oil seeping through the vents.

He grabbed the chair at his table and wedged it beneath the doorknob. Then he pushed the table against the already wedged chair, praying the extra weight might hold his room door closed—false hopes, for false prophets.

The boy was out there; the man had seen his face in the crowd. He'd come for him.

The man emptied his flask in one long gulp. Then he grabbed his pen, notebook, and flashlight and moved into the bedroom's closet, slamming the door behind him. He slinked to the floor, bracing his legs against the door with his back against the wall.

"The pouch!"

He patted along his waistline and sighed in relief when he felt it was still there. He didn't know why he still clung to it.

With no windows in the closet, there would be no escape. It would be his tomb.

It started with human ignorance, our contempt at the idea of forces we couldn't conquer. The germ is us. As each new person got infected in the beginning, one vicious mauling after another, it became apparent our primal selves were no longer inhibited. Weren't we already heading down that path? Neighbor against neighbor. Those in need were spit on by those who weren't. The "others" brutalized by the "superiors." Biological forces were culling the herd.

The protein only seemed to get stickier with time, craving not just the brain but all human tissue down to blood cells and DNA. Nobody was safe.

My neighborhood was overrun in a matter of days. We made the fatal error of treating this like a normal pandemic—stay home and flatten the curve—but the infected no longer followed the same rules. Door locks and home security systems were nothing more than window dressing.

Whole cities, including ours, had to be evacuated, and modern infrastructure bottlenecked into a series of death traps as people tried to flee. I was lucky. With my laboratory expertise being flagged as a national security priority, I was provided with air transport, but everyone else had to fend for themselves.

The government tried to help save lives by sending the National Guard door-to-door, but it was all for naught; they were about as effective as flies already captured in a spider's web. They were consumed.

I was able to save my son, but not my wife. My boy was despondent, in a deep state of melancholy at having to face our new reality in a refugee camp within our country's own borders.

I found blood on his leg as we exited the helicopter, and his jeans were torn. It was like my heart had been ripped from my chest.

I told him it would be okay, spreading my sermon of hope and salvation. There was no proof I could save my son, but I sold him the box of goods anyway.

I made a cut, hoping to excise the infected flesh to save him. But I did not realize in my panic that I'd grabbed the scalpel: patient Zero's scalpel.

I had it, you see, the scalpel. The government brought it to the medical lab I'd worked in, hoping our team could study the proteins and find a reason for their accelerated consumption, but we didn't have enough time. The infected came and swarmed our walls, overrunning us. In the chaos of evacuating our office, my colleague handed me a neoprene pouch. "Guard it," he'd said. I barely registered the words or had a moment to consider the object I'd been given. Attaching the pouch to my belt, I'd forgotten about it. Until the moment, when I saw it in my own hand, with my son's blood glistening on its blade.

His brain transmogrified within an hour despite the incision being on the calf. He'd become one of them.

His fate was my fault.

In my hubris, I believed I could reverse what I thought he was condemned to. Making that cut was so easy; it was so small...

God, it was me who was at fault. It hadn't been a bite from another infected person that I'd seen; it was from a tick. I found the insect burrowed in the flesh I'd removed after he'd started to go mad.

If it weren't for me, he may still be my son, my warm-

blooded child. I would still be able to hear his laugh and see his smile, but no, I infected him.

I'd wanted to end it, pushing him from the top-floor window myself. But like so much else, I failed. Despite the fall, his mindless body survived.

And now I've seen his gaunt, skeletal face haunting the fence line. After all this time, he still waits, and though I know intellectually that the infected don't travel far from where they became infected, I can't help but feel that he knows his condemner remains here.

If you are reading this, then at least my account of what happened is out there. I don't know if this will help anything, but hope is all any of us have until it runs dry. Mine has.

The gunshots have ceased, and the infected will soon find me. They will die eventually; this disease doesn't truly zombify. Cannibalizing will run its course before they all finally stop, but I will be among them. I will rejoin my son.

They are at my door now. I can hear the hinges squeaking under the force of their blows. This is my end.

He dropped the pen as he heard the wood of his room's door give way, the grating of the table and chair being shoved aside thrumming on the other side of his final barrier of safety as the infected invaded his sanctuary. He only had moments to consider what was coming.

The top half of the closet door splintered, a bloodied arm partially visible in the newly made cracks above his head.

The man slipped his hand into the pouch tied to his belt and removed the scalpel. Its blade shone in the flashlight's artificial illumination and glinted like a polished tooth, deceiving in its cleanliness.

His motion was smooth with the precision of a practiced hand as the blade bit into his skin.

Blood, a vibrant shade of red, washed over him as the closet door finally gave way.

The man's eyes blurred as the infected descended, limbs reaching in and sliding him effortlessly across the blood-slicked floor. Then two decayed fists bunched his shirt and lifted him up. He gasped, his final breaths weak, as a face materialized inches from his.

The clouded eyes of the man's son bore into him, the boy's mouth open and releasing a deafening scream that arrested the man's heart. His son lunged, teeth bared. The man was gone.

EXCELLENT HANDS

"My poor little kitten," she said, pulling back the bedsheets to position herself beneath them. "Ol' Nancy will make it better." She wiped her hand across the man's brow, gently removing the perspiration. His breathing was labored, and the last vestiges of life glimmered in his eyes.

Elation flooded through her, and she gripped his penis. It was time.

Phlegm gurgled in his throat as he convulsed and struggled to get air, his body twitching to her cold touch. She rubbed more vigorously, her cheeks flushing.

A clatter in the hallway heightened the thrill, egging her on. Nancy thrived on the possibilities of life, death, and discovery.

She shivered with delight.

Nancy threw her head back as the sheets rubbed against her like unseen hands, tickling her as she wrapped her legs around the prone man and began to thrust, feeling him slip inside her.

All the joy and relief her medicinal cocktails could bring, a sweeter concoction than any martini. Five nights past, the man beneath her had checked into the hospital with a heart murmur. A condition of concern but not fatal—that is, until Nancy got to him.

Her cocktail was an art she had perfected slowly and methodi-
cally over the years, giving doses to her wards until they achieved that
perfect state, the limbo between this world and that of the Almighty,
while Nancy watched, the rush of pleasure moistening the space
between her legs as her patient's eyes dimmed. A splash of morphine
and a shot of atropine pulled them in and out until her breaking
point, where she delivered them to their Maker in a gush of orgasmic
pleasure.

It was more than a labor of love for Nancy; it was her calling—the
one thing that could satiate her. After five nights of doses that took
the man to the brink of mortality, a catatonic state that was a hairs-
breadth from the end, it was time for Nancy to quench her thirst.
She'd primed her desires during that time, watching the man's eyes
grow vacant as she edged on the line of euphoria until she couldn't
handle it anymore. She'd acted, giving the man his final dose.

Nancy crossed herself with one hand while bucking her hips,
digging her pelvis into the man's shrunken penis. It contracted as the
life left him, sliding out of her, but she wouldn't be deterred. She was
so close.

She grabbed his chin, forcing him to meet her eyes, moaning
softly to herself. His gaze was a glassy nothingness, giving her, and
her alone, the last glimpse of his soul.

"Amen," she whispered, leaning her head back and sighing, a
mighty whoosh that left her lightheaded.

A tingle of pleasure radiated from her neck down to her toes as
she caught her breath, the moistness between her thighs releasing in
a stream. She reveled in it, slowly lowering her head down to the
pillow and rolling off him.

"Rest now, poppet. Nancy made sure you won't hurt anymore,"
she said, wiping a tear from under his eye. The moment had been so
beautiful and tender, which Nancy rarely encountered. Many
patients go too quickly or thrash about violently upon their final
dose, but every once in a while, there is that one who transcends their
final struggle to connect with her in their moment of death. He was
one of those lovelies.

Throwing aside the blanket and covering her plaything's body, Nancy stood and felt goose bumps flourish along her naked legs. The window had been left open, allowing in the frigid, early winter air.

Sometimes the staff has no sense. What if someone caught a cold?

Nancy slammed the window shut with a sniff of irritation before returning to the bedside. Her toes tingled as she slipped her boots back on, that last remnant of the thrill fading. It would come again; it always did.

She laid the syringe back into the thin medical pouch, nestled between the delicate vials containing her cocktails, and began to secure it, tying it against her inner thigh with a tattered strip of cloth. The package made Nancy who she was, and she prized it more than her own life. It gave her access to death, that sweet delicacy that filled her.

With her pouch securely tucked beneath her shift, Nancy pulled her rough gray nurse's dress back over her head, followed by her white apron and bib. She adjusted her hair and white cap just so, determined to appear just as she had when she arrived.

Nancy smiled at her reflection in the window and let out a high-pitched giggle that sounded like it belonged to a child rather than a grown woman.

Time to clean up.

The room was sparsely furnished, with a metal-framed bed and an old wooden nightstand. Most patients had beds packed together in large halls, but she was lucky enough to get assigned to the second floor, where the wealthy got private rooms—a place where she could give them her undivided attention.

She wiped the man down with a rag from the bucket near his bedpan. The water was cold, but he was past the point where comfort mattered. Once she had done this, she adjusted his nightgown to adequately cover him and pulled the blanket to his chin, resting his hands peacefully atop his chest. She needed to ensure there was no sign of her presence, or she could risk everything. Nancy couldn't afford that.

"Perfect," she said, approving of her handy work.

Her deed done, Nancy approached the door, listening to the squeaky wheel of a passing nursing cart.

"Knock, knock," a distant voice said, and a door opened down the hall with a squeal before thumping closed. Nancy waited until there was silence for several moments, letting her know it was safe to proceed.

After adjusting her nurse's apron, she entered the hall, closed the door softly behind her, and headed toward the nurse's station. The floor was silent except for the clicking of her heeled boots, the sound echoing through the corridor as she walked; the faint odor of her ejaculation wafting up to her nose intermingled with the twinge in her popping hip.

Nancy felt old then, remembering all the patients over the years and the inescapable end they each met, her hand flexing at the thought of depressing her syringe. She loved every one of those patients in her own way, each serving an intimate moment with her that led her to divinity. For who else was able to usher them to their eternal sleep, watching their eyes grow dim forever? Her cheeks grew hot at the thought and she could feel the rush of blood that signaled her arousal.

Cool down now. We're no hussy. Let's honor the dead first, she thought, trying to force down the urges after having just released with the old man whose body wasn't yet cold.

A child's scream erupted in a room off to Nancy's left and a fellow nurse approached and entered.

What a dreadful noise. She better quiet that child down or I'll have to pay a visit.

Nancy's mind wandered to her brother. He could never sleep properly either, but she solved that. Her father questioned her at length before he fell ill himself. Before Nancy started caring for him as well.

"What happened, Nancy? You were alone with him? You said the army doctors taught you this was safe!"

She understood her father's emotional outburst when he had come home that fateful night so many years ago to find her brother not breathing. His insomnia was too great, and Nancy had yet to perfect her cocktail for someone so small. Lord knows she tried; her pleasure was disrupted over and over by her inability to drug him properly, bringing him just to the brink. She lost her patience on the final attempt.

"Just sleep, my darling," she said behind feigned tears as she jabbed the syringe into his arm and depressed the plunger, releasing enough morphine and atropine to kill an adult, let alone a child. "My poor little bunny." He had been only eleven, her father's only son. The light left his eyes almost immediately, leaving her disappointed and unfulfilled, her arousal all but instantly doused.

"I gave him the right amount, father. He was looking a bit pale... I think it must have been something else."

Her brother's death had been ruled a heart defect, and her father became bedridden soon after, unable to banish that image of finding his son lifeless. His heir was gone. She helped him the best she could initially, but Nancy began to have cravings once more, fantasizing about that final moment of ecstasy when she could watch his eyes cloud as he transitioned out of this life, her fingers rubbing between her thighs. It was beautiful.

Nancy's brother and father weren't her firsts, however. She'd received her training from the best of them, working in the medical unit with the US Seventh Cavalry at the battle at Wounded Knee. She saw the bullet wounds, the flowing holes in the flesh that couldn't be stanched, their only salvation being a drug-induced twilight administered by the medics.

It was a holy experience, her hands the difference between suffering and tranquility, the quivering of their bodies stimulating something inside her that brought her to climax.

In the army, she was able to hone her cocktails, testing them without consequence as many of the men had no hope of survival. If Nancy lost a few patients, it was deemed the inevitable end due to the severity of their wounds. It was perfect, allowing Nancy to learn just the right dosages to cause a seizure, a convulsion that would make her weak in the knees until she was ready to tip them over the edge, not to mention comas and death.

She'd wait until night when the unit's staff was sparse, enough cover for her to insert the men into her, to truly feel the end with them. Nancy had tried to have sex in a traditional manner once long ago, but it brought her no pleasure; the grunting, sweaty dominance of a man, the near-immediate end with no satisfaction for her. No, the only way, the true way, was at their moment of ascension to the one on high with her in control.

Nancy flushed as she saw the old man's face again in her mind's eye. She shivered and ran her hands over her dress and apron, trying to smooth away any signs of what she'd been doing.

She reached the counter, where weary expressions from fellow nurses met her as they discussed the recent tuberculosis outbreak. The ticking clock, moving steadily like a beating heart awaiting her care, welcomed her instead.

"Hello, Betty dear. How is Mr. Calloway this evening?" she asked, motioning her head back the way she had just come.

Betty looked back at Nancy, her eyebrows furrowed. "What? Didn't you check on him yourself? You just came from that way." She was always looking at Nancy like she was doltish. There was a reason for that: Nancy played dumb well.

"Why no, not yet, my sweet, but I have a quarrel with someone. As I've been making my rounds, I've noticed that the windows in some of the rooms have been left open again. Someone is going to take a downward turn from a draft."

Betty flinched and shifted her gaze toward her fellow nurses at the station. Nancy thought she was probably mulling over that silly accusation. The nursing shortage ensured that coincidental deaths wouldn't affect her employment. As long as she covered her tracks and painted suspicion elsewhere, Nancy would be safe—that and not lingering for too long at any one hospital.

"We will be sure to look into that, Nancy. Carol is making the rounds now, so I'm sure she will pop in on Mr. Calloway soon. As for you, there is a new mother over in room 18 in the maternity wing who needs a check-in. Why don't you head over there," said Betty, her steely gaze sparing no warmth for Nancy.

She knew that Betty didn't trust her; veiled accusations and snide comments became a regular thing for her after three of Nancy's patients died within three weeks of each other. She'd had to smother her cravings and resist doling out her cocktails in the hospital for nearly a month afterward to quash any scrutiny. Luckily for Nancy, she found a home-care patient to tide her over, a childless old woman she could take her time with and savor.

Nancy felt goose bumps along her arms and legs as a rush of delight coursed through her.

"A new mother? What a joy! I'll head right over," Nancy said, giving Betty a saccharine smile. Betty and the other nurses exchanged glances.

Nancy wandered away without a second thought.

She'd always steered clear of the maternity ward. Children never gave her much joy, especially a colicky one. They served a purpose, however: an opening.

Nancy's sister kept her distance from Nancy after their brother and father died, but three years back, she had to overcome her reticence and ask Nancy to move in and help. The poor dear needed a caesarian for her third child and the incision hadn't healed right. A live-in nurse was the only solution, and Nancy was the only one she could afford, as Nancy asked for nothing more than a room of her own. After a five-week stay, they all perished, save Nancy. Authorities later determined her sister had complications from her procedure, and the three children had contracted cholera. They each died with their eyes open and as blank as undeveloped film; such an unfortunate coincidence.

"Hail Mary, full of grace," Nancy began reciting as she crossed herself, her smile growing even wider as she remembered touching herself while watching their eyes in their death throes. "Amen."

Nancy entered room 18, and the exhausted mother was propped upright against pillows, holding her new baby to her breast as nursing aids cleaned the afterbirth and feces off the end of the bed.

"A new baby. What an absolute delight!" Nancy said enthusiastically, clapping her hands. "Let me help you, my dear."

Nancy retrieved the baby and laid it in the arms of one of the nursing aids who would escort it to the nursery. The mother moaned in pain as blood continued to seep from her. A bead of sweat rolled down her pale, plump cheeks, eyes glistening with tears.

Meeting the mother's gaze, Nancy's cheeks flushed as she felt a stirring of arousal. She knew she needed to stay vigilant with Mr. Calloway just passing and Betty being ever watchful, but she couldn't pass on such a ripe opportunity.

Just a few days of peering into her soul, savoring the dimming of her light... Then, that final dose. Nancy shuddered, feeling the pleasure all the way down to her toes. *Yes, this will be the last, and then I will switch to another hospital—I'll resign that night. Three more days for that final thrill and then I'm gone.*

Nancy sat beside the mother and brushed a hand along her cheek.

She looked around casually before slipping one hand under her dress, along her inner thigh to retrieve her concealed treasure.

"Let me give you a little something for the pain," Nancy said.

She took several draws of different vials before flicking the tip of the discolored syringe and moving the small medical pouch to the bedside tray. A gentle melody drifted across Nancy's lips as she cinched the woman's arm with the cloth she used to secure her pouch in place and injected her cocktail. A loud bell from the hallway joined her tune with a mighty crescendo, and Nancy needed to grip the woman firmly to prevent her from moving too much, startled by the noise.

"Oh dear, someone must have passed," Nancy told the mother as she heard the nursing aids outside the room run off to discover the source of the commotion.

"Shh, there, there," Nancy said, bringing her mouth to the mother's ear as her eyes started to close and she began to shiver.

"Nothing to worry about, my dear. You are in excellent hands."

PART THREE
DAWN

TOTALITY

K ill me, Drew thought as he sweated in the baking sun shining through the car window. The air was heavy and thick, oppressive in its weight, like the warm wet towel used after a shave at the barber's. St. Clair, Missouri, in August. This wasn't a destination they ordinarily would have chosen, but it was less flashy than the alternatives. Totality was coming—the Great American Eclipse.

He rolled down the window, the warm air giving little reprieve. His fingers left an imprint of moisture on the toggle switch.

"Damn, it's hot."

Jimmy exhaled from the driver's seat, his unspoken agreement in their collective discomfort. Stray grass peeked out along the train tracks, which ran parallel to the freeway. The remaining landscape was barren beyond the occasional tree, a glaring juxtaposition to the crowds flooding the nearby town for the rare celestial event.

Only an hour had passed since they'd left the hotel, St. Louis distantly behind them, and their excitement-tempered patience had begun to run thin. Air conditioning was a luxury taken for granted.

"I wish we took my car—"

"Yeah, I get it, Drew, it's hot."

Jimmy turned on the radio.

"You don't have to be a dick."

"Then stop complaining. I'm just as uncomfortable as you."

Drew brushed his hand along Jimmy's, an apology that couldn't linger; the heat forbade it.

"Sorry I snapped." Drew smiled in response.

"Comedian Jerry Lewis died yesterday morning at his home in Las Vegas—"

"Shh, oh my God. From *Seinfeld*? George's dad?"

Jimmy looked at him, frowning.

"That's Jerry Stiller."

"Oh... Well, that's still sad."

"Yeah," Jimmy trailed off. He couldn't help wondering if they should have stayed back in town. On their way out, they'd pulled off at the grocery store, a small shop with a few snacks and an abundance of eclipse-viewing accessories, not to mention beer. He was sure fighting for a spot would be nearly impossible. Large tents and congregations of cars already littered the store's parking lot and nearby park, tailgating—the favorite pastime on steroids, eclipse edition.

But here, outside of town, crowds were no longer a problem. Rather, the lack of public space was the issue.

They pulled off the freeway onto a pothole-laden road in desperate need of repair. They crested a small hill that opened to a smattering of homes, private land, and the occasional American flag. They were trespassers in a part of the country that was foreign to them, and the unease started to creep between their shoulder blades.

"I have to pee."

Drew nodded.

"Me too. See anywhere to park yet?"

"Over there," Jimmy pointed toward the railroad tracks. "I see an empty space on that gravel. We can park there, I bet."

Drew shrugged. "Works for me."

They weren't the only ones to have that idea. Within minutes of pulling over, several other cars joined them.

Jimmy climbed back into the car, having to cut off midstream.

"Do we have an empty bottle?" Jimmy asked, voice bereft of amusement.

"Only if we dump out some water."

"Fine, would you? What a waste."

Handing off the emptied bottle, Drew climbed out and looked around as Jimmy maneuvered into the backseat to finish relieving himself.

The occupants of the caravan of vehicles waved at Drew as they all got settled. A light breeze caressed the hair on his arms, carrying the hot, oily smell of asphalt with it.

It was 12:26 p.m.

"About forty-five minutes to go. Are you excited?" Jimmy asked, his voice having shed its irritation. He put on his solar-viewing glasses, his head focused upward, and got out of the car to stand beside Drew.

"You can see it a little bit."

He handed Drew his glasses. Their hands lingered with one another for a moment, a subtle squeeze. Then a car door slammed, and Jimmy dropped his hand to his side. Gay marriage may have passed two years ago, but the Pulse nightclub shooting followed it a year later. Moves toward justice are often met with reactions of injustice. They knew this place didn't have the anonymity of the city, the liberal bastion of home.

"This is so cool. I remember an eclipse from when I was a kid—kindergarten, I think. I didn't have glasses, so I couldn't look at it."

"Well, I'm glad you were smart enough not to blind yourself," Jimmy said, still looking upward. "It isn't any darker. I wonder when it will start setting in?"

"At totality, I presume," Drew replied.

Jimmy nodded in agreement. He got his phone out and told Drew to keep looking up as he took a selfie, immortalizing the moment.

"Well, I don't know about you, but I'm thirsty," Jimmy said.

He took off his glasses and walked back to the car. He poured a can of hard cider into a plastic cup for each of them before taking the lid off a veggie tray from the grocery store.

"Oh, do you want a snack?" he asked Drew teasingly, holding the tray out the open door.

"When am I not hungry? Open the hummus, too," Drew said as he approached.

He leaned into the car to retrieve it from Jimmy, sneaking a kiss.

"Did you get a kiss?" Jimmy asked, grinning.

"Mhmm."

Jimmy sat in the passenger seat and finally relaxed as they waited. The air was no less warm, but the pressure of finding a place to settle was alleviated.

Drew walked around the car, propped open the driver's side door, and sat, eating from the tray as if famished, while Jimmy drank his cider just as steadily.

It was 12:33 p.m.

"Huh," Drew said, unlocking his phone screen.

"What?"

"Just an alert. A bunch of animals went berserk at Idaho Falls Zoo."

"What does that mean?" Jimmy asked.

Drew shrugged. "I'm not sure. It doesn't say anything about injuries, just 'this story is developing,'" Drew said, air-quoting with his free hand. "Hmm, there are also a lot of bats in numerous locations along the line of totality, I guess. Don't animals do strange things during an eclipse?" Drew asked.

"Do I look like I work here?"

Drew frowned at Jimmy, who was staring back at him, expression utterly devoid of emotion.

"Smart-ass," Drew said.

"What's that?" Jimmy asked with a smirk.

Drew shook his head and continued to scan the article.

"That's out West. There is practically no wildlife in Missouri, so I'm sure we'll be fine. Don't worry about it," Jimmy said.

"Aren't you forgetting about the Ozarks? They have wildlife," Drew replied, frowning.

Jimmy shrugged and stuck his head out the passenger door. He looked up at the sun again. "I'm starting to see it more."

They got out of the car and looked upward through their glasses. They could see a slight sliver of darkness creeping over the sun's western edge.

"Looks almost like the Apple logo, doesn't it?" Jimmy asked.

Drew made a huff of acknowledgment, nodding his head.

"Hiya! Where are you all from?"

Startled, Drew looked down to eye level to see a woman close by in a bright red shirt waving at them; her kids were setting up lawn chairs a short distance away, moving as if the slightest delay would result in them missing the entire eclipse.

"Chicago," Drew said, uneasy at being approached by this stranger.

"Oh, wow, you came far. We drove over from Doolittle. Can you believe this spot? How lucky, huh? It's filling up as much as every-where else, though. We stopped at least a dozen times before this."

Drew nodded his head, his eyes following the length of the rail-road tracks. Cars lined them, some even closer to the tracks than the space they had found. People packed themselves into every nook and cranny they could find. The remoteness of the setting seemed to recede as a sensation of something otherworldly crept in—a nomadic people chasing an astrological sign of untold fortune.

"Yeah, I can't believe how many people there are," Drew replied.

Another group of people pulled up next to Jimmy and Drew and started setting up their viewing site. They already had their viewing glasses on as they worked, looking like they were entering a 3D cinema.

Suddenly, Drew felt a jolt.

"Put your phone away and take a look up," Jimmy said.

"Hmm?" Drew rubbed his arm and shifted his gaze to Jimmy.

They locked eyes.

"What's going on?" Jimmy asked.

"I'm getting a weird vibe," Drew responded.

"Something is going on, I'll admit," Jimmy agreed.

"Yeah..."

Drew picked up his cup, finished the last of his cider, and leaned into the car for a refill. He waved his hand gently above his empty cup to keep the bees from landing in it. The bees were plentiful and persistent in their pursuit of sweet human treats, moving in small clusters between the groups of people around him.

"Want more?" he asked Jimmy as he cracked open another can.

"Obviously."

Drew smirked.

It was 12:44 p.m.

Drew felt his phone vibrate in his pocket.

"This is getting weird," Jimmy said, slowly lowering his phone after trying to take a picture of the eclipse with it, his eyes transfixed on the screen. "There is a mass riot of prisoners at Natrona County Jail and the Juvenile Detention Center."

Drew sniffed. "And I'm supposed to know where that is, why?"

"You aren't. It's in Casper, Wyoming. Strange things are happening along the eclipse's path, which is my point," Jimmy said.

"I told you something wasn't right earlier," Drew said.

Jimmy waved him off dismissively as he continued to read.

Drew shuddered and looked around at all the people surrounding them. Sweat ran down his back like cold fingers in the oppressive heat, taking his breath away.

"How much longer?"

"Totality is in about thirty minutes. We aren't by a city, so I'm sure we'll be fine. I wonder what the hell is going on, though?"

"I'm not sure, but—J, I'm starting to get a bad feeling about this. Maybe we should leave."

Jimmy lowered his phone and stared at Drew. His tone was clipped and riddled with irritation.

"You're joking, right? We drove all the way from Chicago and paid for that hotel on top of everything else and you want to cut it short because of a few weird instances happening in confined spaces? It's not like this is happening in the middle of the streets. They say weird things happen during full moons, and you don't hide under the bed during those."

"Jesus, fine."

"Well? I'm sorry, but you are overreacting a bit," Jimmy said.

Drew took a deep breath, partially to calm his fears but also to suppress his frustration. He needed Jimmy to understand him—it was their age-old argument.

Jimmy took off his viewing glasses, his eyes softening.

"We'll be okay," he said, his voice reassuring.

Drew nodded, countering his natural inclination and trying to convince himself Jimmy was right. He couldn't shake the chill, though, like the reaper's hand on his neck—something intangible and just out of sight, but nevertheless present.

Drew forced a smile. "Yeah, of course. I've seen too many movies."

"Aww, are you crazy? Yes," Jimmy said playfully, rubbing a hand along Drew's face.

"Piss off," Drew replied, trying to suppress a smile.

"We need Gaga, and you'll be fine."

Jimmy reached inside the car and turned on the radio. Lady Gaga belted out "Bang, Bang," muffling the hum of nearby conversations from the other spectators.

"Well, this definitely won't draw attention to us being the gays along the tracks," Drew said.

Jimmy smiled. "Oh, you think you're funny?"

Drew smiled back as Jimmy started a subtle choreography to the song, not too obvious but enough to take the edge off and have a little fun. That was the point, after all, for getting away from the city for the weekend—to escape the grind and endless noise, to watch a natural phenomenon in a place of low energy, and to find their Zen.

Drew looked around, letting the jazzy notes of the song flow through him. People near him were doing the same, with drinks in hand, laughing and conversing, viewing glasses on, and preparing for the show.

The blazing sun overhead was constrained, and their surroundings were muted as if looking through a tinted window. Drew could feel the coming storm, whether by instinct or visual acuity, as the world around him darkened under the cloudless sky, that sepia-toned and elusive dread in his periphery.

He wiped a bead of sweat from his brow.

It was 1:01 p.m.

> 1:01 PM
>
> Are you watching the eclipse? How is it out there?

Drew put his phone back in his pocket. He would feel the response, so there was no reason to hover. Jimmy had turned down the music and was looking skyward again.

"If I put a pair of these over my camera lens, do you think it could capture it?" he asked, already attempting what he'd just asked was possible.

"Here, use my glasses to try it so you can look up at the same time and see what you're doing. I read somewhere that the light could damage the sensors without protection, so it's probably the only way we should try to get an eclipse photo anyway."

Jimmy shrugged, then took Drew's glasses and put them on.

Bzz-bzz.

Drew unlocked his phone.

> CHRISSY
> 1:02 PM
>
> Yeah! Are you?? It's so weird how dark it got. We came inside because Tom saw a bat, and Ella was getting bitten by mosquitos—like, what the hell, right?! There are freakin' fireflies outside! You would think it was dusk.
>
> Anything like that happening by you??

> 1:03 PM
>
> Nothing here yet. I'm in Missouri, so we still have a few minutes.

Drew shivered despite the heat as he put his phone back in his pocket. Chrissy was hours away in Lincoln, Nebraska, yet only minutes away celestially. What was happening out there? Bats? Mosquitos? Fireflies? The nocturnal fire and blood sweeping the arc of the solar full moon—what did it mean?

The cider tasted bitter as Drew took a long drink, pagan superstition clawing at his sensibilities.

"Hey, I got one!"

Jimmy held his phone out for Drew. In the photo, the moon covered more than half of the sun; they had approached their event horizon.

"Wow, that's great, honey. I can't believe you were able to get it."

His voice was hollow to his ears, riddled with insincerity.

Jimmy frowned. "Are you freaking out again?"

Drew sighed and slumped his shoulders. "Maybe."

Jimmy slid the viewing glasses back onto Drew's face and grabbed his chin, lifting it skyward.

"This might be the only time you see this in your lifetime. Focus on that."

The weight of those words sunk in as Drew saw the penumbra in the sky above, the ball of Newton's cradle passing a torch on its invisible string. But what force was being released?

"J, it's almost time!"

"There you are. That's the spirit I was looking for. Isn't it amazing?" Jimmy asked.

"It really is..."

Drew trailed off as the eclipse neared totality, the moon fitting snugly into place over the sun like a key in its designated lock. A hush descended over the onlookers as everyone turned their attention upward. The breeze settled as if suppressed by a new gravity, forcing genuflection to the eye in the sky.

There was silence.

It took a moment for them both to realize it, but the birds had stopped chirping. A solitary hoot from an owl interspersed with the distant chorus of crickets were harbingers of the approach of the artificial night.

Jimmy grabbed Drew's hand and squeezed it. The contact of his skin felt clammy; whether it was with excitement or fear, Drew couldn't tell—perhaps both.

"This is surreal."

They looked at each other, unable to hide their grins.

"I love you," Jimmy said.

"I love—" Drew broke off as his phone vibrated. He looked at it.

Message Failed to Send.

He frowned. The message to Chrissy had been trying to send for nine minutes but to no avail. Drew clicked "Try Again," and the green status bar moved across the top of the screen. It froze halfway despite the icon indicating the phone had full cellular service.

"There it goes," said Jimmy. Drew looked back up as the moon finished sliding into position.

It was 1:12 p.m.

The light fled, like turning a dimmer switch down, plunging them into twilight rapidly but not instantaneously. They looked out toward the horizon, shifting their focus to take it in panoramically. They could see light off in the distance, a capped sunset, rays peeking out like the bulb in the refrigerator reaching through the crack right before the door closes.

"Should we take off our glasses?" Jimmy asked.

Drew shrugged. "Okay."

They removed them together and looked up. Their fear of everything that had been building as the eclipse approached was wiped away by their sheer awe of the glowing ring above them, the halo of darkness and majesty. Despite the day's heat, the stillness brought a chill, yet the creeping dread they'd both felt with totality's approach had melted away. Nobody spoke, taking in the universe's visual statement of supremacy.

"Wow," Jimmy said, mouth agape.

Drew looked around, and others were doing the same, as if in a daze. There were no birds, just the sound of crickets. The incessant buzzing of bees had been replaced by swarms of mosquitos, a hoard of them following the train tracks like blood through a vein, surrounded by a human buffet ripe for tapping.

"It's so calm," Drew said, catching Jimmy's eyes in that exact moment. He couldn't remember the last time he'd seen such wonder on Jimmy's face, like that of a child that touches grass or sand for the first time, registering the feeling, the scent, and the sight. He grabbed Jimmy's hand and looked skyward again.

"Just a minute left."

A black blur flew past them, but they were too distracted to register what it was. Its wings carried it in spurts, up and down, rather than the graceful line common of the avian rulers of the daytime sky. And it wasn't alone. More of the small, furry, black creatures appeared, diving toward the trees or brush, flapping their way toward the rhythmic pulse of dozens of heartbeats, summoning them like a dinner bell.

In the twilight, the winged creatures swooped in on their prey from behind on quiet wings, pulling them along. It was synaptic, inducing a pack mentality as creatures bit humans, in turn leading the bitten to strike the next closest person, feeding the colony in a domino effect of bloodletting.

Their bites were stealthy and swift.

It started along the edge, one bite after another rippling through the crowd, teeth and nails accompanying the fangs of the creatures. Then the human victims continued the feast, scratching and digging their fingernails into the flesh of their neighbors, silently pulsing forward in a hedonistic flurry of vampirism.

Oblivious to the onslaught, Drew flinched, the feeling of invisible fingers moving more deliberately down his spine; the reaper, just out of his view, reaching for him. His breath caught. Listening, he heard the light shuffling of people behind him and knew he must be overreacting. He had to be.

Jimmy squeezed Drew's hand, the clamminess even more pronounced now.

The sanguinarians crawled over the tracks as if metamorphosed from being human into something feral, carrying their winged passengers to the other side on their shoulders. Their actions were nearly soundless, like the assassin's knife, as they latched on to one new victim after another and continued devouring the crowd.

The woman in red opened her mouth to scream as her children sunk their teeth into her calf, but she froze as her warning reached her lips, sensation fleeting as if given procaine. Her dilated, iris-less eyes fixed on Jimmy and Drew.

She moved, creeping like a cat on the hunt while the little winged creatures fed from the wound on her leg. Her hand led the way, groping the air before her, fingers curling into a claw, nails straight, a garden rake poised to split the soil.

Saliva pooled in her mouth.

She could taste them.

So close.

She raised her hand above her head, veins and tendons protruding, a rheumatoid talon fixed in position.

She could smell their cologne, their fear. She could...

It was 1:14 p.m.

Then a diamond formed in the sky. A flash so bright along the edge of the moon that Drew's and Jimmy's eyes began to water before they could look away from the eclipse.

"Ouch," Jimmy said, wiping the tears away.

Drew put on the viewing glasses and looked back toward the sky, basking in its immeasurable beauty. The sun really did look like a shimmering diamond, pushing away the dark like a lighthouse in the night. He could feel the reaper's fingers retreating, the shadow in his periphery burrowing further and further into irrelevance, with each passing second.

Jimmy tried to take another photo through his glasses, knowing it had been a day to remember.

"Did it work that time?"

"Eh, can't tell," Jimmy said, shrugging.

Drew took his glasses off. "We should probably get out of here. The traffic will be hell," Jimmy said.

"You don't want to take it in anymore?"

"Oh, so now you want to stay? I told you nothing would happen."

"Is that a no?" Drew asked, watching Jimmy walk to the driver's side of the car.

"Sometime before my next birthday," Jimmy said, motioning for Drew to join him.

Drew rolled his eyes. As he turned around to walk back to the car, he noticed that the woman in the red shirt was a few feet behind him. Her leg had a gash on it, and her eyes were unfocused. He flinched, taking a step back.

What was she doing so close to him? He felt a knot of fear clench in his belly. He cleared his throat.

"Are you okay?" he asked, keeping his distance.

She looked at him, squinting. Her irises were dilated, and she seemed confused.

"Um, what—I mean... yes? I think I fell."

Her movements were loose and wobbly, feet not planting right as she took a step.

"I think she's drunk," Jimmy whispered, reaching out the open window, grabbing Drew's arm, and tugging at it.

"I'm... I'm fine. It was nice meeting you," she said, before turning around and wobbling back to her children, who also seemed dazed and stared blankly at the horizon.

"Drive safe," Drew said, getting into the car.

"Yeah, so, let's get the hell out of here," Jimmy said, putting the car into drive.

Dirt kicked into the air as they pulled away, creating a thick brown cloud that masked their exit. People milled around aimlessly, staring in their direction, all with squinted eyes.

"Did we miss out on the drugs or something?" Drew asked, puzzled.

"We're in the country, honey," Jimmy said, deadpan.

"Right."

Nothing terrible had happened to them after all, but something still wasn't sitting well with Drew. His gut told him—*Oh, screw it*, he thought.

He reclined his seat, getting more comfortable as the temperature rose with the re-exposed sun.

"I'm going to take a nap."

"Good idea. Traffic will be awful, so let's switch in two hours. Getting home is going to take a while," Jimmy said.

"Okay. I love you."

"Love you, too," Jimmy replied.

Drew kicked off his shoes and curled his feet to the side. His heel poked into the darkness below the seat, rubbing against something soft. He thought it must be a sock and closed his eyes.

Nothing terrible had happened to them after all.

AFTER THE RESCUE

"Hello, Rapunzel. How are you feeling today?"

Rapunzel sat in front of me in a regal blue gown, her long, blonde braid thrown over the back of her chair and curled into a pile atop a velvet pillow on the floor. She met my gaze, her eyebrows creased. She was tired. I'd have to be a fool to miss that.

"It's been hard, Doctor, but each day gets a little easier," she said.

I nodded. The poor girl had been through so much throughout her life. First, she was locked away in a tower with no parents and nobody to love or guide her. Then, a harrowing rescue by a prince turned her life upside down and plunged her into the spotlight of royal intrigue. That wouldn't be easy for anyone.

"Tell me more. Are your dreams troubling you again?" I asked.

When she first came to me, urged to do so by the Prince, she was the embodiment of how a princess should appear—poised and opulent—but something lingered behind that mask of how she presented herself to the world: a certain wildness.

She wasn't a tame creature; she was used to doing what she wanted when she wanted to do it. Alone in that tower, who would have denied her? But her destiny was to be the rescued maiden and to marry the Prince; the whole land knew of the legend. And after jailing her captor, an old witch who'd had a few too many ales before foolishly trying to jinx—unbeknownst to her—an off-duty palace guard in a pub for his pouch full of silver, the royal family knew exactly where to find her.

Her rescue was truly something out of a dream, and that's what she told me during our first session. We've held onto that theme, every description of her chaffing at her duty being described through the lens of a dream. After weeks of tough conversations, it was time to break through.

She watched my hand, my quill at the ready above a piece of parchment. Rapunzel waited, holding the silence.

She never made things easy.

I put my quill down and heard her let out a breath, her shoulders rolling back into a relaxed slouch.

She cleared her throat.

"I wish it were so easy an explanation as that," she said. "If it were a dream, I could wake up and avoid it until my next sleep. No... no, this is much worse. My dreams have now become my refuge."

Well, that was new. What an interesting turn this has taken. Her dreams had been a source of so much anxiety for her, so much unhappiness and expectation, or so she'd alluded to—but now, to call them a "refuge"?

"This is quite a change from before, Rapunzel. Let's delve deeper. Tell me about your life at the palace. What do you need refuge from?" I asked.

She sighed, rolling her eyes to the side in distress.

"It hasn't been what I expected, Doctor. I've given it time, with your help, of course, and I appreciate Her Majesty's generosity, the clothes and jewels, the elegant ball, but the Prince..."

She closed her eyes and took a deep breath to calm her nerves. Where was this going? While my duty was to my patients and their health, I, too, had an oath to the crown, with which I walked a fine line to keep confidentiality. I couldn't push her too far; some things I wouldn't be able to hold back from the royal family.

"Please, Princess, continue," I urged.

She nodded, opening her eyes. They held a spark, a new resolve.

"Is this just between us, Doctor? I need to get this off my chest, but I'm unsure how to handle it quite yet."

I nodded slowly and moved my parchment and quill to the side table. Even with my reservations about what I could truly keep confidential, I couldn't let that show. Rapunzel needed to see me not only as her therapist but also as a confidant, someone she could trust to unburden herself. I had no desire to betray the girl.

"Yes, you can trust me. That is my purpose here: to be a sounding board for you and to guide you in navigating this transition," I said.

I'd hoped she'd already known she could trust me, but her caution wasn't unwarranted.

She nodded, a slight upturn to the corners of her mouth. Was she grinning?

"Does your clinical advice hold any weight with the royal family?" she asked.

I frowned. The royals relied on me quite heavily for recommendations of mental fitness, often seeking my seal of approval before condemning someone.

"The royal family trusts my opinion on an array of topics related to mental health, whether it concerns members of the house or criminals awaiting sentencing. Why do you ask?"

She leaned in conspiratorially, lowering her voice.

"It's the Prince, you see. I don't think I am what he wants. Nothing I do pleases him. I was hoping for a recommendation from you stating that I need some time away from him, from my royal duties, for reflection—"

"Princess, this is highly irregular. I can't make such recommendations to the royal family without cause. Explain yourself," I said. I was flabbergasted. What woman would want to distance herself from a prince?

Rapunzel sat back in her seat, her face sullen and pouty.

"If I must."

With each step she took forward in her treatment, she almost immediately took two steps back. I sighed at her petulance, but I had to remind myself of her beginnings. She needed to learn her place, and that could take time.

I circled my hand in the air, a gesture to continue.

She adjusted a stray piece of hair that had loosed from her braid, sweeping it away from her face.

"Well, you see," she paused, eyebrows scrunched, "my alone time in the tower had always been a curse, or so I thought. Night and day, I was alone, reading the musty tomes left in my single room in that tower—stories of gallantry and princes who always came to the rescue of the damsel. But you see, Doctor, I've always had a brave heart. One must develop something of that, being alone, never knowing when a man might make his way up to my window."

I smiled. How silly I felt and how relieved I was. She was just scared of men. I could talk her through that adjustment.

"Ah, but you know the story, Rapunzel. They needed your golden hair let down to make it up to you. There was nothing to fear."

I felt a pang of unease when she leveled her gaze at me as if I were the unschooled pupil and not her.

"Men with arrows and grappling hooks had come close more than once, Doctor. I had to learn to defend myself."

"Did anyone actually make it up to your window?" I asked.

She moved her head, a nod so subtle I hardly registered it.

"Once, but I'd learned what to do long before."

She looked at me again, eyes hard like ice.

"I dealt with it," she said.

I rubbed my chin and leaned against the seat back. I had hunched forward, anxious for her answer. This young woman had seen far more than I would have suspected.

The Princess cleared her throat.

"Anyway, eventually the Prince came, calling out for me to let down my golden hair. I did so as the tales prescribed, and he whisked me away to the palace. Our journey was long, you see, and we had to spend many nights camped along the roadside. It was my first real experience with a man."

I gasped, causing her to stop suddenly. The Prince couldn't have.

"Had the Prince known you carnally before you were wed?" I asked, my voice full of shock.

She looked at me a moment, at first startled, and then her face changed to amusement.

"Carnally? Me and the Prince? Ha, heavens no," she said, her face conveying what she thought of my foolishness. "I merely meant I experienced the brutishness of a man firsthand. The passing of gas, the urinating on everything as if no better than a hound, all his lewd comments; it was savage."

She let out a laugh, her face contorted in a sneer at the hopelessness of her situation.

"By the time we reached the palace, I knew that living with a man would be horrible, but what other choice had I been given?"

She slumped her shoulders in defeat. I was dumbfounded.

"But don't you love him?" I asked, struggling to figure out how to proceed.

"What is love, Doctor? Is it something learned or something known? So many fairytale stories describe this magical feeling of love at first sight, but I... I felt I was better off in my tower."

I frowned. This just wouldn't do. The Queen would want this rectified immediately. I had to convince her otherwise for her own good.

"Now, Princess, you must enjoy his company. He is the Prince. He is handsome, rich, well-mannered, and heir to the throne. Surely you must see what an honor this is."

She rolled her eyes, and I felt my frustration begin to simmer. I'd thought we had been making progress in recent weeks, but now she was back to acting no better than a child.

"Actually, no, Doctor, I don't see. He's nice to look at, I suppose, but he's a savage!"

"Princess, that is enough. You cannot speak of the Prince this way."

She eyed me wearily.

"The Prince has many wonderful qualities you haven't allowed yourself to see. I am giving you lots of leeway with what you experienced in your youth and your time alone, but do not be foolhardy. You cannot speak of the Prince so harshly; it's not like he hurts you." I stopped speaking, realizing I had been lecturing. I was supposed to be helping her, but I had become someone no better than any other royal stooge.

She met my gaze. Her eyes still conveyed a stubborn resolve. I needed to get back on her side.

"What I meant to say was, he doesn't hurt you, right, Princess?"

Her hand swung up in the air, and she let out a laugh.

"Don't make me laugh, Doctor. He wouldn't dare lay a hand on me."

"Oh," I said. I was utterly confused.

"I've seen the two of you together. You both appear to enjoy each other's company."

"Isn't that what's expected, Doctor? It's been made clear that I 'must do my duty.'"

I nodded. Yes, we'd all made that abundantly clear.

"Part of that duty is to give him an heir, Princess. You balked at the idea of knowing the Prince carnally earlier. Are you saying that holds true, even now that you have been married for the better part of a year?"

She froze, eyes wide, a signal I read as me having gone too far, but then she let out another laugh so bitter and seemingly full of malice that I cringed.

"Do you think I would touch that thing? I told him the first time he presented it that I would remove it if he exposed it to me again."

"Truly?" I asked, nonplussed.

"Am I a bitch waiting for a stud to mount me? Of course, *truly*, Doctor."

I sighed and shrunk back into my chair. I had no idea how to reach her.

"But the Prince rescued you," I said, low enough that I didn't expect her to hear it. This would cause a royal crisis. The kingdom would have been better off if she'd never been found. Maybe following through on her request that I recommend she take a break would be the best thing for her.

My clock's alarm started to ring.

She cleared her throat.

"I believe our time is up, Doctor," she said, standing and smoothing her skirts.

"Yes—yes, of course," I said, standing and grabbing my quill and parchment.

"Before you go, please allow me to apologize, Princess. Perhaps some time alone, reprieved of your responsibilities, is what you need, to consider the gravity of your duty to the crown."

She tried to suppress a smile.

"Does that mean I can go back to my tower? I'd require my lady's maid come with me this time, of course. So I can maintain my studies of civilized society."

"But, Princess, your lady's maid is my daughter. Surely you can't think I'd want—" I cut off suddenly as the full gravity of the situation became clear.

For years, I'd had to make excuses about why my daughter couldn't come to court, from illness to lack of civility, even going so far as to besmirch her name by saying she was simple, being only worthy enough to be a servant, willing that reality into being. But none of this was true. I was trying to protect her.

All those years ago, when she was barely considered a woman, I'd caught her in a kiss of passion that should have never been. If anyone had found out about her inclinations, I'd have been ruined.

Rapunzel stared into my eyes and nodded, her smile no longer restrained. She knew what I was thinking about.

"I believe we now understand each other, Doctor. I'll see my way out."

The Princess sauntered out, hair dragging behind her like a mighty serpent, leaving me alone, mouth agape.

FLASH

It's not every day that your life flashes before your eyes.

It happened so suddenly, the steering wheel turning one direction and then the other, my arms working to correct my trajectory as I lost control, the inevitable catastrophe fast approaching. It all happened in the blink of an eye, the realization followed by that stab of fear in my gut, that dread.

I can't fix this.

Tires squealed, and the pungent smell of burning rubber flooded my nostrils as the concrete median approached.

"Oh God!"

The moment of impact was eerie, a *Matrix*-style slow motion, while in reality it happened in seconds. My heightened awareness took in everything: my phone falling to the passenger-side floor, my muscles bracing to the point of pain, the visual onslaught as the front of the car pancaked, and the airbag bursting forth, covering my line of sight with a concussive blow.

I gasped, the air pushed from my lungs as I was thrown forward into the tensed seat belt; little white specks, like static, blurred my vision as the airbag finally made contact, forcing me back into the seat.

My heart was racing, and my mind couldn't catch up to what was happening. I had no control. Whatever happened was out of my hands.

Seconds ticked by, but it felt like minutes, time losing any meaning. How could one process so many stimuli in a mere flash? I tried to find peace, convincing myself that I'd made it through, but a force was still pushing against me, and it was then that I realized I was still in motion, this time going in the opposite direction.

The speed at which I hit the wall made sure to follow the law of physics, using the excess energy to push the car backward. My hands were still clenching the wheel in a vice grip, and it was then— whether from clarity or defeat—that I let my hands slide to my lap. There was nothing I could do.

I turned to the left, watching the world move around me like in a movie. The visuals didn't register as the dangers they posed, the other cars, the flashing lights, none of it, until that one horn, clear and distinct like that bellowing echo heard at sea on a foggy day, broke through.

"Oh shit!"

A red and monstrous semitruck barreled toward me, its hood beginning to angle downward as the force of its brakes tried to stop its mass, the driver's-side door being the only barrier between us. Other cars were blaring their horns, swerving out of the way to avoid their own disasters, and the semi had nowhere else to go but forward, with me careening across its path.

It has been said many times that when near death, a person's whole life flashes before their eyes, pops of memory playing in their mind's eye like a movie projector, but I didn't experience this.

Instead, I watched the feature of a life that may never come. My daughter's first dance, dressed in a gown her mother wore for her first homecoming, standing nervously beside her skinny date with braces. Her graduation from college, standing at the podium accepting her degree from a white-haired professor. My tenth wedding anniversary, standing arm and arm with my wife, looking up at the Eiffel Tower. My mother holding her first great-grandchild as my daughter sat in the foreground, finally understanding the love we'd always had for that little life she had been. Everything that could have been but would no longer be possible for me as the candle of my life was extinguished...

I closed my eyes, clenching them shut, hoping it would be like the flip of a switch: no pain and instant.

I felt a jarring thud behind me as something made contact with the car's rear. I held my breath.

I heard nothing save for the noise of cars passing by.

I opened my eyes.

The semi crept by after our near collision, a lion eyeing the gazelle now safely out of reach. I didn't understand as I looked from left to right. My car was backward in the shoulder, the trunk up against the concrete median, the very one I had hit head-on just moments before.

"I'm alive. Oh my God, I'm not dead," I said, my voice coming out at a swift pace as I reached for the overhead visor. Tremors raced through my arms, my nerves finally catching up with me. I visibly shook as I opened the mirror and peered at myself.

I was there. I'd really made it.

"I'm alive!" I yelled, letting my head hit the headrest with enough force to give a slight bounce on impact.

I'd never faced death before that moment, living life like its rules didn't apply to me. I wasn't reckless or anything, but death hadn't seemed applicable. I'm sure everyone young feels that way until they face the stakes.

That movie, all the unmade memories, began playing for me again; the quality lessened as it faded away, like going from 4K resolution to trying to pick up a show with an antenna, but it was enough for me to see it.

I had another chance. I'd get to hold my daughter again. Those glimpses were still possible.

The tears came on their own, and I noticed their wetness on my cheeks before registering the emotions bubbling inside.

I wiped them away, but it only made it worse. More tears

appeared, like condensation on a glass of ice water on a hot summer's day; they wouldn't stop forming.

I sat that way for quite some time, sobbing and grateful, as the police arrived and diverted traffic away from the left-hand shoulder where my car sat.

There was a knock on the car window. It was a police officer.

"Do you have anyone you need us to call for you?" the officer asked.

I nodded as I felt additional tears roll down my cheeks. "My wife."

I buried my face in my hands, and in what felt like moments, the car door opened. A hand caressed my shoulder, causing me to look up. It was my wife, her face full of fear but also relief at seeing me unharmed.

Oblivious to the aches and pains that would settle in my body later, I climbed out of the car and wrapped my arms around her, feeling her warmth and heartbeat. Feeling life.

"I'm alive."

STARDUST

"What should we do for dinner tonight?"

"I'm not sure," Brian said.

Every night, they had the same conversation, the parley of the day. It's not that they fought regularly—far from it—but marriage is a perpetual state of give and take, with someone always deferring to the other. When it came to dinner, Shane usually extended the olive branch.

"It is such a nice night out... maybe takeout?" he asked.

Brian shrugged. It's not that he didn't care; he was just indifferent. The air was warm, and they could finally enjoy being out of the house, putting minimal mental energy into anything else. After another day filled with one mind-numbing Zoom meeting after another, he felt lucky that he didn't have to think about breathing.

"Ramen?" Shane asked.

"Sure."

"Oh, what about tacos?"

"I literally just said sure to ramen," Brian said, gesturing with a sideways flip of his hand, though Shane, looking at his phone, didn't see.

"Did you hear me?"

"What? Maybe burgers? This place looks good," Shane responded, scrolling through pictures of various burgers on the restaurant's Google Maps entry.

Brian sighed.

"It doesn't matter."

Shane ordered the ramen and they got up to put their shoes on. Crossing the street to head into the thick of Wicker Park felt like being in a game of *Frogger* as cars continued to speed by despite them being in the crosswalk.

"Get me out of here," Shane said as they moved deeper into the neighborhood, away from the chaos of Milwaukee Avenue. The sound of cars carried on the breeze, a swirl of life after a period of silence. The pandemic had brought everything to a halt, and city life had become overwhelming as it all tried to start back up again.

"I don't know if I can get used to that."

"What?" asked Shane.

Brian nodded his head, gesturing toward the noise behind them. "The traffic and the noise. I'm so overstimulated."

Shane smirked, putting his hand on his husband's shoulder. "You'll get used to it again. I think we all have a lot of recovering to do."

Brian raised his eyebrows and nodded in agreement.

They turned a corner and a couple jogged past them, wearing masks. Mandates may have loosened, but some habits would take a while to shake.

House-shaped shadows stretched across the street as the sun descended in the west. All along the street's length, to the next intersection, people were sitting on their front steps, an amalgam of humanity needing the fresh air.

As different as the people were, so were their homes, with some being remodeled, others newly constructed, and even more divided into cheap apartments. This was the embodiment of gentrification, but for once, there didn't seem to be any conflict.

Laughter and conversation pulsed along the street, powering it like the third rail on Chicago's "L." Families and friends drinking and eating, refusing to let slip away the life the virus was meant to stop.

"This is COVID waiting to happen," Shane said, angling his steps on the sidewalk to widen his berth away from the people and closer to the street. Brian looked at him and then back at the pockets of socialization, several people making eye contact and nodding a weary acknowledgment.

He sighed. If only his husband could enjoy this moment after so many of theirs had been taken by this global catastrophe. Trips, time with family, their honeymoon... *Just enjoy the walk*, he thought but didn't say.

"I'm sure most of these people live together," Brian said, following Shane with his eyes.

Shane shrugged.

"Yeah, well, this is how it spreads. Hopefully, they do."

Noticing Brian's irritation, Shane stepped closer to him and lowered his voice. He cleared his throat and bobbed his head over his right shoulder.

"Look at her," Shane said.

Brian knew Shane was trying to change the subject, but he played along anyway. He turned his attention to the homes on his right.

An older woman sat on the front steps of a two-story row house. It was run-down, with cracked shingles and chipped shutters. Brian couldn't even tell what the original color should have been. The woman sat alone, her face distant, eyes not focusing on anything.

Shane shivered.

"What?" Brian asked.

"It's just her energy."

Brian rolled his eyes.

"Shane—"

"You know that I can feel people's energies, honey. I'm very in tune."

Brian sighed.

"So you've said."

Brian loved his husband, but he was a storyteller and an embellisher. That was part of what he loved about him, though, at times, it was also his biggest irritation.

"I know you don't believe me, but I can read people. Everyone lets off their own frequency of energy. We're all just stardust."

"Like the Force?" Brian asked, not interested in giving this conversation any more steam.

"Oh, you think you're funny?" Shane asked. His expression held no amusement.

"Okay, fine. What are you feeling from her?" Brian asked. He wasn't going to die on this hill. As much as he didn't want to hear them, he'd let Shane tell his stardust theories.

Shane moved closer to his husband, speaking low and conspiratorially.

"Sadness. Loneliness. It's almost like she comes out here looking for companionship and... well, nothing."

"You feel all that? It *is* a pandemic. Everyone feels alone. Maybe she lost someone, or they are sick. We can't know," Brian said.

Shane glared at Brian.

"Regardless, I can feel her melancholy."

Brian scrunched his eyebrows and looked Shane in the eyes. He was so sure of himself.

"I don't know," Brian said, doubt creeping into his voice. Shane took Brian's wavering in his certainty as a rare win.

"Trust me, I know what I'm talking about," Shane said, smirking.

As they continued walking, Brian turned to look at the woman again. She looked lost, and as she stood and turned to go back inside the house, all he could feel was pity for her. He wanted to run to her and ask if there was anything he could do for her—a hug, something. But the door shut behind her.

Shane may have been right this time.

THE WOMAN BLINKED the sun out of her eyes as she walked over the threshold.

"There you are! Where did you go?" a man asked.

The woman shook her head, dispelling her bewilderment. Her husband stood in their kitchen, a smile that had illumined her soul for the last thirty-six years on his face.

"I was just out front. I needed—" The woman paused, shaking her head. "I needed some air. I still can't believe it."

"Well, believe it, baby! We actually won. Think what this means," the man said, raising his fists above his head in triumph. "The kids. We can pay off their college and retire somewhere warmer like we've always wanted. I just—"

Tears formed in his eyes, a well of frustrations and struggles on the brink of being released. They'd both worked multiple jobs, relying on their eldest daughter to watch her siblings since they sometimes could not be home for hours at a time. No matter how much work they put in, it never felt enough, and they were never paid what they were due.

He closed his eyes, and the tears released, rolling down his cheeks. The woman could see the weight lifting off his shoulders.

"Fifty-five million dollars, though... I still can't believe it," she said.

Her husband wiped his eyes with his sleeve and put his arms around her.

"When you put good energy out into the universe, good things happen eventually. It's written in the stars," he told her as he touched his forehead to hers.

They kissed, and she wiped another tear from his cheek.

"I guess you're right."

CITY NIGHTS

The air was dense, the moisture slick on every surface. Chicago summers in late July, hell on Earth, unless living in a sauna is a preference.

The breeze, a rare visitor in this sweltering landscape, was like a precious droplet of water in a desert. When it did grace the cosmopolis with its presence, it was a welcome respite, nature's oscillating fan, gently swaying the oppressive curtain blocking the window, allowing a fleeting glimpse of the treasured sky.

The sun began to set, birds chirped, and cars drove by, as mixed in their state of repair as the surrounding neighborhood, just on the cusp of gentrification.

Flags of all shapes and sizes billowed from their windows, pronouncing the pride of their heritage as scattered caravans of vehicles navigated the city's thoroughfares like cells in the bloodstream, the essential piece of life.

The neighborhoods were a symphony of sounds, a cacophony of late '80s to modern rap music blaring from passing cars. Each vehicle was a burst of noise that eventually melded into the sounds of the native landscape: the clanking of bicycle chains, the hum of conversation—some hushed, some boisterous as couples exchanged heated words from window to sidewalk—and always the distant hum of the metropolis... the wail of a siren, the thump of a helicopter, and the constant drone of the interstate.

The sun disappeared, replaced by an indistinct sky, our own projections repelling the universe's display. New stars twinkled to life as the community adapted to the darkness, balcony gatherings illuminated by strings of manufactured light. Laughter, tears, and reminiscences filled the air, a collective reflection on what was and what could have been, a shared breath in the solitude of the night.

The city endured even though the sun had faded. Whether a virus or upheaval brought the premature darkness, the certainty always remained that another day would come. There would be light again.

Afterword

Writing a short story is an interesting endeavor, requiring all the concentration involved in telling any story, condensed into a smaller package that must be just as satisfying as its long-form counterpart, the novel, complete with character progression, climax, and resolution—it's not as easy as it sounds.

When I first started writing short stories, it began as an exercise in scene writing. I would have a flash of inspiration, jot it down, and *BAM*, I thought I had a short story. Sounds nice, right? Unfortunately, I quickly learned that I had great buildup to something—all the action one could hope for—but there was never a resolution; the scene just stopped. It took me years of trial and error, and most importantly, practice, to finally understand how to refine that little lump of a story into some form of a diamond (I can't exactly say how shiny it is; that is your job, dear reader). The fourteen stories in this collection are just a few of my favorites that I decided to share from that journey. Some of these are twelve years old, while others are no more than one, but within this little collection, I was able to group together a thematic journey that, while dark at times, I hope left you with a glimmer of hope for the possibilities tomorrow can bring, despite any number of horrors you might encounter along the way—oh, and I hope I entertained you too!

As most people have heard, writing is a solitary venture, and I can attest that it is true. There have been so many moments when I wanted to set the computer aside and play Mario Kart with my daughter, watch a new show with my husband, or even just take a nap, but my stir-crazy mind wouldn't let me; I had a story I felt needed to be told, and I couldn't feel settled until I had it down on paper. This compulsion required sacrifice of our most valuable commodity: time—well, that and it tested the patience of my family. That said, I owe them the biggest thank you for supporting me and understanding that I needed that space to work toward my dream of writing. So, Justin and Graysen, thank you; I love you both more than I can possibly express in words.

Next, I can't forget my cheerleader since I came screaming out of her womb (unfortunately via a cesarean), my Mom. Almost every time I talk with her on the phone, she asks how my writing is going and tells me how proud she is of me, and of course, as moms often do, when I'm hard on myself, she'll say, "honey, you will do it," with never a hint of doubt in her voice. Mom, thank you.

I also need to thank my editor, Sheila Loesch, who has opened my eyes to so many details I'd never considered in my writing. Sheila has been instrumental in asking me the tough questions that have pulled my best ideas to the forefront, and I know my work would have been lesser without her.

And lastly, thank you to Caleb Thompson and Kandice Hart, my fellow writing mates who have been with me for most of my writing journey, as well as my best friends Jordan Chelovich and Kendall Schultz, who have inspired and supported me since we were in the fourth grade—thank you for keeping me somewhat sane!

To sign off this afterword, I need to thank you, dear reader, for believing in me enough to read this book. I hope the journey you had with my characters will bring you back for more of my stories in the future. Until next time!

ABOUT THE AUTHOR

Chris Kauzlarich is the author of the horror short story collection *Menagerie in the Dark* and the novellas *LAZARUS* and *Moody Road*. A member of the Horror Writers Association, the International Thriller Writers, the Authors Guild, AWP, and the Chicago Writers Association, he writes dark fiction that unsettles precisely because it lives so close to home. A graduate of Purdue University, Chris lives with his husband and daughter between Chicago, IL, and Naples, FL — or somewhere on the open road in their RV, where the best and worst ideas tend to find him.

To stay updated with Chris and discover new books, connect with him on social media or sign up for his newsletter at chriskau zlarich.com.

facebook.com/Writer.Chris.Kauzlarich

instagram.com/chris.kauzlarich

goodreads.com/kauzlarichcı

amazon.com/author/chriskauzlarich

threads.com/@chris.kauzlarich

bookbub.com/authors/chris-kauzlarich

DID YOU LOVE THIS BOOK?
CONSIDER LEAVING A REVIEW

I hope you enjoyed *Menagerie in the Dark: Stories* by Chris Kauzlarich. If you did, would you leave a review? Nothing helps an author more than readers spreading the word so others can discover it as well.

Please use the QR code or website link below to leave a review on Goodreads. If it isn't too much trouble, could you also leave a review at the place where you purchased it? I will be eternally grateful :)

Thank you again for your support, and happy reading!

https://www.goodreads.com/book/show/233715543-menagerie-in-the-dark